SEBERIAN™
THE GREAT GATE

"Open their eyes and turn them from darkness to light, and from the
power of Satan to God."
Acts 26:17 NIV

J.R. DAHL
SEBERIAN.COM

DEDICATION

This book is dedicated to all those who
fight to protect life and freedom.
They are soldiers of hope, Seberians.

Lonan

- Mechanical engineer of the planet Helion (specializing in aerospace & aircraft design)
- Husband of Averine
- Brother of Sevran
- Childhood friend of Telgrin

Averine

- High-ranking medical officer in the Helion army (Field medic)
- Daughter of Kilgron
- Wife of Lonan

Kilgron

- Supreme commander of the planet Helion
- Long-time warrior in the Helion army (severely wounded in battle)
- Father of Averine

Sevran

- Commanding officer of Helion Army Field Medical Units
- Brother of Lonan
- Childhood friend of Telgrin
- Single and very popular with the ladies of Helion

Telgrin
- Mechanical engineer of the planet Helion (specializing in weapon and transportation systems)
- Socially awkward but brilliant engineer
- Classmate of Lonan at Helion Military Academy

Maginon

- CEO of Nemaron Corp

Devakin

- Ruthless commander of Leviathan army
- Powerful and experienced warrior

Armon

- Commander of Seberian forces
- Long-time warrior
- Father of Ahren and Cloin

Ahren

- Young leader of Seberian Forces
- Powerful, disciplined warrior, especially gifted at covert operations
- Son of Armon
- Brother of Cloin

Cloin

- Young leader of Seberian forces
- Incredibly focused and intelligent warrior, especially gifted in hand-to-hand combat
- Daughter of Armon
- Sister of Ahren

Nemaron

- Intergalactic corporation that sells rare minerals and essential commodities

Leviathan

- Mysterious supernatural army

Seberians

- Small, elite, supernatural force of humans

Helienders

- Soldiers of the planet Helion

Satan

- Demon, former angel (Angelic name = Lucifer)
- Chief of all demons
- As an angel one of the nine chief (or "arch") angels

Mammon

- Demon, former angel (Angelic name = Mammelel)
- Direct subordinate to Satan while they were angels

Abaddon

- Demon, former angel (Angelic name = Abadol)
- As an angel one of the nine chief (or "arch") angels

Abadile

- Demon, former angel (Angelic name = Abafrile)
- As an angel one of the nine chief (or "arch") angels

Tekel

- Chief (or arch) angel, one of the original nine
- Strongest and wisest of the angels
- Commander over all of God's faithful angels

Balim

- Chief (or arch) angel, one of the original nine
- Guardian over galaxies 55x5 through 78x35

Genon

- Subordinate angel
- Had been a direct subordinate to Satan before his fall
- The only angel under Satan's command to not succumb to temptation
- Was direct witness to the beginning of war in heaven

A Word
from the Author

This book you are about to read started as a movie script. We're on an amazing adventure of producing it as a feature-length film. I wrote this novel adaptation of the screenplay in order to get the story out into the world and start creating an audience.

The story is intended to communicate Biblical truth about the reality of our fallen world and the hidden spiritual battle that rages all around us, the battle between God's faithful angels and Satan and his legions of demons. In spite of the fact that the story is about spiritual warfare, the angels and demons are not the focus. The humans and their struggle in the mist of this battle are the focus of the Seberian series.

The task that I believe God has given me in writing this story is to show how Jesus was the Messiah and what he did when he came to earth. 1 John 3:8 says that Jesus came "to destroy the devil's work." (NIV) I want this story to show how his victory over sin and death affects us and what impact it made in the spirit world.

My heart for this film and story has always been that it would be a movie that Christians would enjoy but also that it would be a cool sci-fi movie that we could invite our non-believing friends and family to see. Something that they would enjoy that would then spark good conversations about the content. The message of the story essentially has two parts. First, that God is for us, not against us, and that He still acts in this world. Despite the fact that it's fallen and messed up, He still loves us and fights on our behalf. The second part of the message is that we have an enemy who is out to destroy us. But the good news is that we have victory over that enemy through Christ.

I chose the science fiction genre as the platform to tell this story. First of all, I *love* science fiction and have done so all my life. I think the beauty of using this type of genre is that we can retell a story in a way that parallels the original but has a fresh or unique twist on it. That allows the audience to experience that story in a new way that will hopefully impact them. Unfortunately, some of our Christian teachings can sometimes get misunderstood or seen as cliché because they have been heard over and over again, which in some cases causes them to lose their meaning. For the non-believing world statements like, "Jesus died for your sins," could be really confusing. They may have heard it many times but never made the connection between one man dying two thousand years ago affecting their lives today.

My hope and prayer is that this book and movie project can follow in the footsteps of great Christian thinkers and writers like J.R.R Tolkien and C.S. Lewis. They proved that science fiction and fantasy can be used to communicate Biblical truth while entertaining the audience at the same time. I don't think that we can ignore the fact that things like movies and music impact our lives, particularly in our younger more formative years. I believe that this story could be a positive source of hope and light, particularly to our young people.

Our goal is to produce and distribute the film independently. That might sound crazy, but with changes in technology for both production and on-line distribution it's very much a realistic goal in today's environment. Not only is it possible but it would also be much safer for a movie like this. In the wrong hands the message of the story could be taken in the wrong direction. So thanks to advances in technology in everything from digital cameras to free open-source animation software, we don't have to go and beg Hollywood to do it. And most importantly we can maintain the integrity of the story.

If you would like to be a part of making the film a reality, or you're just curious about the progress, please check out our website, **SEBERIAN.COM**. There you can sign up for our email newsletter in order to stay up to date. We call the newsletter *The Seberian Nation*. When you signup you can get access to free downloads like the novella prequel: *Seberian, The Beginning*. We do not sell or share anyone's emails so you will only be getting messages from me, Jason Dahl, about this book and movie project.

One final thing that I would like to share is that twenty percent of all book sales goes toward helping to cover adoption costs for families who are in the process of adopting a child. Many things triggered the writing of this movie script and novel series, and one of those was five years of infertility which resulted in God building our family through the miracle of adoption. That money goes to a special fund that was set up by the organization that we worked with to complete our adoption process. It is set aside to cover families specific adoption costs and not general overhead. It also does not go directly to individuals but is distributed through the agency to certain families as needed.

We call this the "Soldier Of Hope Campaign" and we are honored to help other families as they "look after orphans," as James 1:27 says. We were helped by many amazing people in the process of our adoption and we hope to extend that help to others as well. You can find out more about that on our website, Seberian.com.

So without any further delay, I would like to invite you to continue on and enjoy the novel.

Thanks, and God Speed,
Jason Dahl

SEBERIAN.COM

Chapter 1

Here lies the continuation of the story of the battle between Satan and his army of Leviathan, and God's faithful angels and their allies the Seberians. The Helienders have now joined the battle as they step alongside their fellow humans, the Seberians. If you have not yet done so, please read the first in the series, Seberian The Hidden Battle Revealed, and download your free copy of the prequel: Seberian, The Beginning.

SEBERIAN.COM

After the death of Ahren, Armon and the rest of the Seberians loaded his body onto their primary battle transport. Cloin stood outside of the Helion base on the edge of the westernmost shuttle launch platforms. She gazed off into the distance, watching the planet's primary star set on the horizon. This platform was the least used, so she was completely alone and could hear nothing but the wind blowing through the enormous trees that lined the perimeter of the concrete landing platform. This place was peaceful and secluded, which was what she needed. She turned and slowly walked to a nearby boulder and sat down. She wanted time alone to think and to process what had just happened.

She glanced down at her hands and found a little bit of her brother's blood that had not washed off. She rubbed it and tried to get it off. Her mind spun with questions as she remembered the battle in which Ahren had been killed. She thought about the fact that if Genon had not shown up just when he had, she would have also been lying in a casket beside her brother. The odds of these battles where starting to weigh on her. There were so few to fight this seemingly endless army of Leviathan.

She looked up at the bright red and orange of the sunset on the distant mountain range. The color reminded her of the Leviathan chest plates that they tore from the enemy's armor.

"How can he be dead?" she whispered to herself.

Suddenly she sat upright, sensing someone coming. A second later her father walked through the hangar door and out onto the concrete landing pad.

As he drew nearer, Cloin wiped the tears from her eyes.

Armon slowly walked up beside her and gently put his hand on her shoulder.

"You need to come and be a part of the burial."

"I know," she said as she lowered her head and closed her eyes. "I'm ready when you are."

"It's time. Let's go," answered Armon.

She stood, and they slowly walked back into the hanger. The rest of the soldiers were loaded inside and patiently waiting. They stepped into the ship, harnessed in without a word while the pilot lifted off and exited the Helion hanger.

The flight back to the planet Seber was very quiet. Cloin drifted off to sleep and slipped into a dream. In it she saw her brother being stabbed by Devakin. The scene ran over and over again in her head. She tried to stop him, but she could never move fast enough, could never get there in time to save him. Her body felt as though she was stuck in mud. She could never get to him fast enough to save him. She could see Devakin plunge his blade into Ahren's stomach, but she was powerless to help. The dream would start again and again. Each time she was only seconds short of reaching her brother in time.

Then the dream changed. Devakin stabbed Arhen just like he had done in real life. Cloin ran to help and tried to dress his wound, only for Ahren to die in her hands. But this time, after Ahren exhaled his last breath, he lay dead for a moment. Then, suddenly, he jumped and sprang back to life. This startled Cloin in the dream and in real life as she too jumped. She woke from the dream to find herself strapped into her seat on their ship.

Armon saw her jump. "Are you ok?"

"Yes, I'm fine," she answered as she tried to collect herself. She rubbed her eyes and looked out the window and could see their mountain range in the distance. They had just entered planet Seber's atmosphere. They were home.

Back at the planet Helion, Lonan and Averine were still in the medical bay. Lonan had spent the night there, so Averine had slept on a cot next to his bed. Lonan was just waking up as Averine re-entered his room.

"Good morning. How do you feel?"

"I'm ok. It still hurts to breathe, but not as much," answered Lonan as he tried to sit more upright in his bed. He had electronic casts and equipment all over his body. His broken arm and leg were encased in advanced medical equipment that was wired back to a nearby computer console. His torso and ribs were also encased in a device that wrapped around his entire body. All of these were covered in high-tech digital readouts but were also connected to the computer system.

An orderly entered behind Averine with a tray of food.

"Great! I'm starving."

"I'm going to check on your healing progress, but so far everything is looking good," said Averine as she scanned through several screens on a monitor beside his bed. "We can get you out of here by mid-day, and if all goes well every one of your bones will be completely healed in three days. Which means that you'll be back to normal activities in no time."

"Wow! That long?"

"This equipment is healing your bones at a highly accelerated rate. In fact, it's nearly a one thousand percent increase in time and strength. Your body would take weeks to heal on its own without this equipment," Averine explained as she tried not to get too agitated with her husband's apparent ignorance.

"Ok, if that's the best you can do," answered Lonan with a sarcastic grin.

Averine smiled as she turned from the monitor. "Yes, everything looks good. Let's get you fed and out of here."

"Good. We've got a lot of work to do."

"I know," said Averine as she turned back to the monitor.

Back on the planet Seber the wind blew violently and threw the shuttle in every direction as the pilot struggled to land. His target was a ledge on the side of the enormous mountain that towered far above their home. The shuttle finally touched down in nearly a meter of snow. A storm was blowing in from the far side of the mountain. The inner part of the ledge dug into the side of the mountain and formed a cove.

The loading ramp lowered, and Armon led the way as he guided Arhen's body down floating on the stretcher. The Helienders had prepared his body for burial. They had dressed him in an all-white shroud. He was encased in an airtight casket with a clear top that allowed his family to see his peaceful posture.

The wind whipped the snow over the casket as Averine walked beside her brother. The rest of the Seberians followed behind. As they marched across the ledge and neared the mountain they entered the protection of the cove, and the wind and snow lessened. At the end of the cove stood a short cave opening with no door. This was the tomb in which they laid their dead.

The cave opened entered into a small round room. On the opposite wall was a stone door. Armon pushed Ahren's casket in to the room while the two Seberian soldiers worked to pull open the heavy stone door. It was massive, but was hinged on very heavy metal hardware so opening it was difficult but not impossible.

One of them then entered and turned on a large electric lantern that gently lit the entire tomb. It was a small cave that extended into the mountain nearly thirty meters. Each of the walls had horizontal openings cut into the side of them. In seven of these lay caskets with bodies of fallen Seberians.

Cloin and Armon stood to the side as the others lifted Ahren's casket from the floating stretcher and gently placed him in one of the openings. Cloin stared at her brother as if deep in thought as a single tear rolled down her face.

Armon gently put his arm around her as he gazed at his fallen son. His mind was filled with fond memories of when Ahren was a child. In a flood of images he watched his son grow to become a man, then his mind settled on the day he found Ahren and Cloin as orphaned children on the battlefield. Ahren was holding his baby sister as they hid under a pile of rubble that had once been their home.

Armon was overcome with a flood of emotion. He had been so honored to be their father, to step in and protect and raise them when they had no one. But now Ahren was no longer under his care and he had to let him go.

The rest of the Seberians finished placing the casket and gathered alongside Armon. They all stood in silence for a moment before Armon spoke. "We know that we will see him again in heaven. He's far from all the death and suffering of this world."

The other soldiers nodded in agreement and then slowly filed out of the tomb.

Armon and Cloin stayed back for a while. Cloin stepped forward and placed her hand on the casket. She gazed down at Ahren's face as she said, "I know you are right, but it doesn't make this hurt any less."

"I know," answered Armon as Cloin quietly turned and walked toward the door.

After she left the tomb, Armon walked to the casket. He placed his hand on it and gazed down at his son. A lone tear fell from his eye and ran down the glass of the casket. "I know," he said again to himself as he turned to leave the tomb.

Outside the tomb they walked across the ledge to the waiting shuttle. The view on that side of the mountain went on for hundreds of miles. The winds had intensified as the storm continued to roll in from the north. Because of the weather, they decided to stay the night in their mountain home rather than return to the planet Helion.

The ship launched from the ledge and the pilot struggled to keep it level as they left the safety of the cove and entered the storm winds. Within moments they had landed safely several miles down the mountain in the hangar of their mountain home.

As the Seberian soldiers entered their homes, they were greeted by their children and wives. The somber look on the soldiers' faces immediately communicated to the wives that they had lost someone.

The mood quickly turned to joy as the children ran to their fathers and leapt into their arms. The Seberians shed their body armor and turned their attention to the children as they ran off to play.

Cloin smiled to see the joy of the children as they played with their fathers. She and Armon each went to their private quarters to clean up. Later that evening after the children had gone to bed, Armon gathered Cloin and the rest of the Seberians in the library. He closed the door as they all took a seat beside the fire.

Armon paced back and forth across the hearth of the fire as he gathered his thoughts. "Before we become deeply rooted in this coming battle, I feel that I must tell you some things." The room was completely black except for the blazing fire, which sent Armon's shadow dancing across the walls. "My concern is that the enemy will find a way to tell you a half-truth before I am able to tell you what has really happened," began Armon. "Over forty years ago I was still living on my home planet in galaxy V59. I had been married to my beautiful wife for eleven years and had been moving quickly up the ranks in our global army. I was commander of twenty units and was developing a great reputation among my commanding officers. Then…it happened." He stopped directly in front of the fire and gazed deep into the flame.

"We were attacked by a force that crept in through shadow. They were able to avoid all our security and caught us by surprise. Once they had penetrated our perimeters, we had already lost. They moved with such speed and fought with a strength that we could not match. As my men and I did our best to defend our home from what seemed like an endless stream of lightning-fast attackers, my wife was taken captive. She was able to fire off a distress signal, which allowed me to track her location. She and two hundred others had been taken captive and were being transported out of our city in ground transports. We tracked them to a large clearing, where they had begun loading them in space shuttles. We laid siege on the attackers and freed some of the captives, but not my wife. She was killed. As she ran to try to escape they opened fire and killed many. I found her and tried to save her, but there was nothing I could do."

Armon stopped pacing for a moment. He lifted his hands from behind his back and gazed down at them. His voice softened. "As I knelt there, holding my wife and staring into her eyes, I watched my future disappear as the spark of life left her eyes. I was speechless. I lifted her to my chest and hugged her lifeless body. The battlefield around me, the death and destruction, meant nothing. My world was ending."

He turned back to face the fire and said, "Then I felt a burning sensation in my back, and everything went black. The next thing I knew I woke up in a pitch black cave. It reeked of decaying flesh and the heat was oppressive. Sweat and blood poured down my forehead into my eyes. There were other men there with me also trying to clear their heads as they were just coming to. I could see a light many meters off. My eyes were still filled with a glaze and my vision was not normal, but it looked like the end of a tunnel. I sat with my back against the hard rock wall as I tried to gather my thoughts.

"My mind drifted back to my wife. I could see her lying dead in my hands. Grief and despair poured over me. The pain was so intense that I thought of ending my own life. That thought sobered me, because I'd never in my life thought such a thing. The warrior in me and the desire to survive took over. I tried to turn my thoughts to my escape, but again despair and hatred rose up in me. A battle stirred in my mind that I couldn't control or understand.

"I decided to try to investigate my surroundings. I groped my way toward the light, stumbling across many bodies. Some were alive, some I wasn't sure. When I finally reached the end of the cave I found it barred with thick, crude metal. The mouth of the cave opened into a vast cavern filled with pools of boiling lava. Above it was a caged arena, suspended over the lava. Men were constantly pulled from the caves and thrust into the arena where they fought for their lives.

"They didn't take me for weeks. Instead I sat there in the cave as my mind and body rotted. I was tortured by the thoughts of my dead wife and our unborn child that she carried. I was filled with nothing but sadness, despair, and hatred. My mind grew so dark that I could see nothing but the blackest darkness even though my eyes were open.

"Then one day they came for me. I was pulled from the cave and pushed into the arena with twelve other men. I thought that I had slipped into a dream, because I began to hear voices. Then I saw them, hundreds of demons flying around the outside of the arena shouting at us. Suddenly their voices became familiar. I realized that I had heard them before in the cave. They had been the voices reminding me of how my wife died. They had whispered how sweet it would be to destroy those who had killed her.

'My mind spun as I tried to take in all that was happening. It was complete chaos. The demons growled and screamed at us to fight and kill. I was attacked from all sides by the other men in the arena. Instinct and rage took over and before I knew what had happened I had killed two men."

Armon turned to face his daughter and his soldiers. He found only shock in their eyes as they leaned forward in their seats, hanging on every word.

"After what seemed like an eternity, we were pushed and pulled out of the arena and down a flight of stairs. Once at the bottom of the stairs we entered a long cave. Men who looked like they were half dead worked on what seemed to be an assembly line. They strapped armor to our bodies. The first was the chest piece. I have told you about this. It was the demonic implant that Satan uses to push his evil into the Leviathan soldiers. I have taught you how to fight these men and rip this chest piece from their bodies in order to stop the flow of his evil power into them. However, I have never told you that I know this because I wore one."

Armon pulled open his shirt to reveal the eight slabs of scar tissue spread across his chest. Cloin and the others looked on in amazement.

"When they put it on me, it was excruciating. It was the worst pain that I have ever experienced. I felt that I would vomit. The initial pain lessened, but it was a continuous pain. The scars have never completely healed, and I can still feel the pain from time to time. It created a strange, hollow feeling in my chest. My mind and body where taken captive, yet I could still think my own thoughts; however, now they were all dark and full of hatred. My eyes were very dark. I could see, but it was if I was looking through a prism that twisted and distorted all that I saw. Things looked familiar, but I never truly recognized anything. It was like a very long, waking nightmare.

"As we continued down the assembly line, they put more and more armor on us. By the end of the line I had become a Leviathan. They took us to another chamber where they trained us. The red chest plate hurt, but it imparted superhuman power that I had never experienced. I could run faster and jump higher than ever before. But as I used this power I could feel it poison my already-weakened soul. Every time I used the power it hurt my body physically, but I learned to function with the pain. The power was like a poison that just continued to spread.

"The power that was now pulsating through us also entered our minds. It commanded us what to do. We could still choose. But the majority of our minds wanted to obey the evil voice. That created even more torment, because there was a small part of me that wanted to escape, that did not want this power and the evil sickness that came with it. The battle within my mind was continuous."

Armon paused for a moment and turned to Cloin and the rest of the Seberians. The look on their faces certainly showed their surprise. Cloin hesitated for a moment and then asked, "How did you get free?"

"We were on a mission that had been particularly dangerous. We had attacked a very advanced planet in galaxy 32X4. One of our rockets had taken out a large building. In the heat of battle, part of that building had fallen on me. It broke my right arm and both my legs. Because of the position in which I was trapped I could not lift the boulder. I was trapped under it for days. None of the other Leviathan came to help me out from underneath the boulder. In the Leviathan ranks, if a man falls behind he is left behind.

"I lay in anguish for days as the fear-feeding power began to fade. With no fresh supply of power, I began to gain some clarity in my mind. But I was still heavily under the influence of the evil that pulsated through my chest.

"Then someone found me. The battle was over and the city lay in ruin, but there was a man. An old man. He walked with a staff that was a reclaimed part of a space craft. He was missing one eye and had a crude metal patch over the empty socket. When he found me he approached without any fear.

"As he approached, the Leviathan a rose in me and I tried to grab him. He was quite agile for an old man who couldn't walk without a stick. He quickly stepped to the side to avoid my attack, and in one swift motion he thrust the end of his staff into my chest plate and just under the fear collector. With great strength he pried the collector from my chest with his staff.

"Blood poured from the holes that had been dug into my flesh from the spikes that anchored the device. I cried out in pain as it broke free. The old man grabbed it and smashed it on a rock beside him. The light quickly faded and went out.

"As I lay there in pain I wondered about the large piece of brick wall lying on my legs. Without a word the old man went to work on it. He placed his staff under the wall and began to pry. The wall outweighed him, and there was no way he would be able to remove it. Then something strange happened. As the old man worked, I saw something move behind him. It was as if cloud or mist had gathered beside him and near the brick wall. Then as the man pried, without explanation, the wall began to lift. Suddenly, as if it by a great thrust of power, the wall lifted from my body and flew three meters to the side. I was finally free."

Download the Prequel for free!

Can you picture it as a movie yet? The story that you're reading started as a movie script and it is our goal to produce it as a film. To learn more about the project please turn back to the "Note from the author," at the beginning of this book.

You can also visit our website,

SEBERIAN.COM and…

- Get a Free download of the Prequel,
- Learn more about the book & movie project.

Chapter 2

Meanwhile, things began to stir on a nearby planet. On a very distant side of the same star system there orbited a small, lush, green planet. It was mountainous and had very few inhabitants. In a completely secluded area there lay a wide, flat valley at the foot of a long mountain range. In the center of this mountain a wide cove opened into the valley. The cove was filled with a grassy field that led down to a shallow stream and beyond that continued the wide valley. Many kilometers off in the distance, on the far side of the valley, lay another mountain range.

At the heart of the cove stood a very large door that had been cut into the side of the mountain. It was made of two tall wooden doors that blended into the rocky mountainside. They had been partly grown over by trees and vines and were very hard to see. The side of the mountain above the door was very steep and covered with heavy vegetation.

The full light of the planet's two moons shown down and lit the cove as if it were daylight. It was a very peaceful and quiet scene as the branches of the trees gently swayed in the wind.

Although it didn't look very impressive, this was the great gate. One of the passage ways that God had made that would allow created beings to re-enter His heavenly realm. It was through this gate that Satan planned to march his army of demons and evil Leviathan men into heaven as he mounted his second attack on God's throne.

This night the sky was clear and the air was crisp. Millions of stars shown bright in the sky above. As the night grew the sky filled with even more light. Suddenly falling stars seemed to converge on the small planet. The light trails from those stars grew in intensity until it looked like the planet was in the path of a deadly meteor shower. From a greater distance off in space the stars could be seen coming from distant galaxies and all converging on this one, lonely planet.

Back in the cove one could see that what looked like stars were not stars at all but were thousands of angels in flight. As they entered the atmosphere they burned with a great yellow light. Not until they slowed and landed on the surface did the intensity subside. Some rode in on massive, winged horses that were covered in burnished-bronze armor. Others flew on their own wings. Each wore the dark bronze armor that they had received in heaven on the day that Satan had tried his first attempt at the throne.

The angels and their armor were battle worn, as they had been fighting Satan and his armies for millennia. Once they landed they gathered in the valley and began to greet one another, some like long lost brothers. Many of these had been assigned to other galaxies and had not seen each other for many years. They were happy to be reunited, but the seriousness of the reason remained. There was a feeling of preparation and anticipation. This was made much clearer when deep black clouds began to form over the mountains on the opposite side of the valley.

The angels all stopped and turned when a clap of thunder rolled across the valley as lightning bolts began to bounce between the clouds. They began to organize themselves and made formations across the grassy plain of the mountain cove.

The Seberians flew through the crisp evening air as they entered the atmosphere of planet Helion. Automated cannons turned and took aim from their hidden bunkers buried in the side of the mountain. They followed the shuttle as it slowed for its landing but did not fire as the automated defense grid recognized the Seberian shuttle.

Inside the space craft Cloin sat in the cargo bay cleaning her brother's blade. She gazed into it as her mind drifted back to times when they were children. Times that were much simpler. She longed for just one more moment with her brother. He had always been her best friend, and now she struggled with the deep void created by his loss.

Armon looked back from the cockpit and saw her deep in thought gazing at the blade. He turned back to piloting the shuttle without a word.

Inside the main hangar of the Helion base hundreds of soldiers ran to finish loading their shuttles.

Just then the Seberian transport hovered down for a landing outside the main hangar. Secondary engines fired to slow their decent, sending dust flying in all directions. The shuttle touched down gently.

Moments later Armon, Cloin and nine other Seberians stepped off the loading ramp and out of the ship. Lonan and

Averine stepped out to the hangar door and walked across the landing pad toward them.

"We've a lot to discuss," said Armon. "The enemy is on their way."

"My father is thinking the same thing. He asked me to bring you to the war room as soon as you arrive. This way," said Averine as she stepped aside and gestured toward the hangar door.

As they walked Armon smiled. "For many years we've been watching over your teams as you completed your rescue missions. We watched from the shadows and fought off any demonic forces as they came too near. We've been impressed with your desire to save those who were powerless against Nemaron and their Leviathan forces. It will be nice to finally truly join forces. I think that we have much to teach you in how to battle our common enemy. Lead the way."

"Father," Cloin said. She reached out and touched her father's shoulder as he stepped toward the hangar.

He stopped and turned toward her. He could tell from the look on her face that she needed to speak with him alone.

"Go on ahead," he said to Averine, Lonan, and his Seberians. "I'll be right behind you."

The group turned and walked back into the hangar. Lonan lingered for just a moment. He dropped his gaze to the floor as he remembered the battle in the forest where Ahren had been killed. His heart broke for Cloin and her loss. Lonan could still see the look on her face when she ran to her brother's side. He then turned and followed the rest of the group into the hangar.

"Father, I need some time alone." She looked down at the floor as Armon reached out and stroked the side of her head.

"I understand. Go. Walk. Pray."

"The pain is still very deep. I badly need God's comfort, but so far I cannot find it. I'll be in the forest. I'll be back before day's end."

"Good idea. Do you want some soldiers to accompany you?"

Cloin lifted her eyes to meet Armon's, and a small smile appeared in the corner of her cheek.

"You know that is not necessary," she answered with a full grin.

Armon smiled back. "I know. Go and walk and be alone with God."

Cloin turned and walked away from the base toward the outer edge of the platform.

Armon watched as she reached the edge of the forest and disappeared into the deep trees and underbrush of the mountain. He thought back to the day that he found Ahren holding his little sister huddled under a pile of rubble in the middle of a war zone. Their inner strength and perseverance had always inspired Armon. His heart swelled with pride as he thought about how strong of a woman Cloin had become. He was also eternally thankful to God for the opportunity to raise Ahren and Cloin as his own children. His heart was broken for the loss of his son, but he would never trade that pain and lose the honor of being Ahren's father.

After a few moments of reflection, Armon turned and followed the rest of the group into the hangar and toward the war room.

Cloin hiked up the steep mountainside, at times needing to grab a tree branch to pull herself along. She continued on for nearly seven kilometers until she came to the small clearing on the side of the mountain directly beside the Helion base. She looked through a clearing in the trees and could see out across the valley for thousands of kilometers. The mountain air was clean and crisp. Cloin sat down for a moment to catch her breath as the air was not only cool but a bit thinner than her body was accustomed to.

She looked around at the beautiful scenery. She was surrounded by large, thick trees whose branches swayed in the nearly constant breeze. Small animals ran through the leaves on the forest floor behind her as three different species of birds flew to and fro overhead.

Cloin zipped up her jacket and pulled her collar up over her neck. She took a deep cleansing breath, and when she exhaled she could see how cold it was in the mountain as she watched the vapor pouring from her mouth.

As she sat on the log she bowed her head and just breathed for nearly ten minutes. She heard nothing but her breathing, the animals, and the wind. The tranquility of the mountain and nature alone gave her a great deal of peace, but she needed more than that. Her heart still ached from the death of Ahren. After a few more moments she began to pray.

"Lord God, why? Why? I need him," she whispered as a few tears rolled down her cheeks.

After a few moments she noticed something: she could no longer hear the animals. She slowly raised her head to see that all the trees were completely still. She could not feel or hear a breeze. As she exhaled she noticed that she could also no longer see her breath. She was surrounded by complete silence.

She pulled herself off the log and knelt with her face to the ground because she knew that she was now in the presence of God.

"Speak, Lord. Your servant is here," Cloin said with her face to the ground.

Suddenly she heard a gentle voice that broke the silence with such warmth that she immediately felt at peace. "Lift your face to me, my child," she heard the voice of God respond.

She slowly lifted her head but stayed on her knees. She saw nothing in the clearing in front of her except a warm, radiant glow that filled the area. Peace and love washed over her and filled her heart.

"I know that you feel great loss, Cloin, but you must know that your brother is safe with me."

"Yes, I know, Lord. I guess that my grief is a little selfish. I need him. The evil of this world is unbearable. I want my brother by my side to give me strength and hope as we fight the enemy."

"I understand that, but you need to rely on my strength. At the same time I know that I created you to be in community. I did not mean for you to live life alone. You still have the other Seberians. You still have your father."

"Yes, Lord."

"The time has come for the number of Seberians to grow. Bring more people to me so that they can enter into relationship with me. The time is drawing near that I will send the Messiah to defeat the work of Satan."

Cloin looked up with a glimmer of hope in her eye.

"I can see that the evil is growing. It is time to redeem creation, and I will send the Messiah soon to begin the process. In the meantime you must remain faithful to me and rely on my strength. The power of the enemy will not overcome you."

In that moment Cloin was filled with great peace. All sadness and fear dissipated in the radiance and power of God.

"What must I do next Lord?" Cloin asked as she bowed her head again.

"Go in my strength. Be a source of light and hope to all those around you. Show the people of Helion the power that you receive from me. I have found their concern and compassion for the weak to be noble. I want them to come to me and become soldiers of hope.

"The evil of this world is growing, and nowhere more quickly than in the hearts of men. I will not be patient with this evil forever. I will send the rest of the army of angels to put a final end to all evil, but first I will send the Messiah to redeem those who would follow and destroy the work of the enemy."

"Yes, Lord," said Cloin as a tear of joy rolled down her cheek.

"Now go, my child. Go and show them our ways and the power that comes from following me."

Cloin slowly raised her head to see that the clearing had returned to normal. The wind was blowing and the birds flew through the air. She knelt there on the forest floor for several minutes as she enjoyed the peace that washed over her. Her strength was renewed, and she felt as though she could defeat the entire Nemaron army alone.

She got off her knees and walked back to the edge of the clearing and sat down on a fallen tree. She didn't want to leave the peace of this place. Moments later a deer and its fawn slowly walked across the clearing and paid no attention to Cloin. The beauty of the scene made it much harder to leave, but she knew it was time to hike back down to the Helion base. Cloin took a deep breath of clear mountain air, picked up her pack, and started back down the mountain.

Chapter 3

B ack in the Helion base, Armon and Kilgron stood in the main council chamber. This was a large, dome-shaped room with a round table in the center and walls that were lined with tiered seating. Averine, Lonan, Sevran and Telgrin all sat around the table, as did the nine Seberian soldiers. Armon and Kilgron stood near the podium, which was positioned near the northern wall.

Armon clicked some keys on a console near him, and a holographic image appeared above the table. It was a globe that represented the Helion planet. As the 3-D image rotated and the computer outlined key geographic elements, Armon began to speak. "We have sensors throughout galaxy 55x9 as well as neighboring galaxies, and we are receiving data that indicates an increased number of Nemaron carrier ships heading in our direction." He clicked another button, and the hologram zoomed out to show all of their galaxy. "They appear to be converging on this location."

A highlighted area appeared a short distance away from Helion and its binary star system. "Here you see the Ruen system. It has just one primary star and only four planets, none of which are inhabitable. The surfaces of all the planets are very volatile with extreme temperature variations. The entire system has a tremendous amount of meteor movement, which causes great difficulty in receiving signals from our sensors. However, all of the data projects the Nemaron carriers to be converging somewhere in that system."

"They are hiding out under the cover of the meteors and gathering forces," said Lonan.

"Yes," answered Armon. "That's what appears to be happening. We can't get accurate readings on the size of the force due to poor signal, but it appears to be a large portion of the Nemaron fleet."

Sevran added, "Each of those carriers normally have hundreds of fighters and troop transports."

"So Nemaron is gathering a large army in the Ruen system," said Averine. "That doesn't look good."

"No. It doesn't," answered Kilgron. "Due to the fact that we just had an attack from what appeared to be a small scouting party, we should assume that we're Nemaron's next target." He clicked some keys on the console, which caused the computer to zoom the hologram back into the Helion planet. It then displayed what looked like tree roots or veins that spread out all though out the upper crust of the planet. They were highlighted in numerous different colors and some stretched very near to the planet's core.

"It's just as the Seberians had warned us," said Kilgron. "They're after our resources. Our planet is rich in many of the elements and minerals that Nemaron has been harvesting and selling. I think that their scouting party was collecting readings on these resources and that it's safe to assume that we are next on the list of planets to be taken captive."

"So our plan is still to free the slaves, right?" asked Lonan.

"Yes," answered Armon. "We must free the slaves in order to remove the Leviathan army power. Then we'll have a far better chance of stopping their forces. I'll send my Seberian soldiers with your teams to fight alongside you. There could be some demons at the camps, and you'll need our supernatural power to defend against them."

Kilgron and the others nodded in agreement.

"I'm concerned about the size of this army that appears to be on its way to your planet. I've decided to travel to galaxy 55x8 to gather reinforcements. We have small armies of Seberians spread throughout numerous galaxies. I'll go and gather as many as I can and then return to defend this place. Meanwhile, the rest of you must free the slaves.

"All of you need to beware of Devakin. He is ruthless, his lust for blood is without end, and he will never stop. He rose up the ranks of the Leviathan very quickly and left trail of dead bodies in his wake."

All the Seberian soldiers seated there at the round table nodded their heads in agreement.

"So the time has come to execute our plans," Kilgron interjected. "Shut down the slave compounds, save the captives, and remove the enemy's power source. I have a quick meeting with the Helion general council, then I'll meet all of you in the main hangar."

After he said this they all stood and walked toward the door. As they did, council members started to enter the room for Kilgron's meeting.

Later, in the main hangar, Armon and the Seberian soldiers were unloading weapons and equipment from their shuttle when Cloin walked through the main hangar door and toward the Seberian shuttle. Without even seeing her Armon could sense that she was coming. As he continued to unload gear from their shuttle he said, "How was your time in the mountains?"

She walked to her father, who then stopped what he was doing and turned to her with a smile. She hugged him. "It was good and very much needed."

"I'm glad to hear that," Armon answered with a smile. "I want you to stay here and help defend their base. I'm going to find as many of our fellow Seberians to come and help. The Nemaron army that's gathering appears to be very large. We need more help."

"Yes, Father," Cloin said. She picked up the last pack full of equipment from the shuttle.

Armon hugged her and then stepped up the loading ramp into the Seberian shuttle. "I'll be back as soon as I can," he said as he closed the ramp and walked to the cockpit.

The rest of the Seberian soldiers stood beside Cloin as Armon fired up the engines and lifted the shuttle up off the landing platform. He waved to her through the cockpit window and then just seconds later was high above the mountain base and passing through the planet Helion's outer atmosphere.

Shortly after Armon left a woman's voice came across the loud speaker. "All personnel report to the main hangar. All personnel report to the main hangar."

Along the innermost wall of the hangar ran a high balcony. Kilgron stepped out onto this balcony as the soldiers all gathered down below. Lonan, Sevran, and Telgrin stood together in the middle of hundreds of soldiers as Averine joined them. Cloin and the rest of the Seberians gathered together behind them.

They were completely ready for battle dressed in their lightweight, black armor.

As the soldiers settled in, Kilgron began to speak. "All of you have your orders, and you know what's at stake. If you do not accomplish your missions, a powerful army will attack our planet with such force that we will not be able to repel them. Many years ago we came to this place and made our home after this army ravaged our home planets. It seems that we can run but not hide forever from this Leviathan army. We must turn and fight in order to defend our new home.

"Our new allies, the Seberians, have informed us of where this army is receiving its supernatural power. They're feeding on the fear, misery, death, and destruction of those they hold captive. We believe that they will begin executions very soon."

Kilgron raised his voice and slammed his fist down on the podium. "We must save the slaves in order to save our planet! We will not run from this army again."

He paused for a moment and scanned the crowd. He was relieved to see confidence and boldness in the eyes of the Helienders. "Now go, and God be with you."

Once he finished, the assembly of soldiers dispersed and ran to their shuttles.

Lonan and Averine walked to his waiting spacecraft. Lonan carried a box of ammunition as Averine delivered one last bag of medical supplies to Lonan's shuttle.

"You *are* staying here this time, right?" asked Lonan.

"Yes! I promise. My father has assigned me here to help protect the base and tend to our wounded," Averine answered.

"Ok. Stay here!"

"I will!" insisted Averine with a grin.

Lonan stepped down off the ramp and reached down to kiss his wife. Averine smiled. "Be careful, and Godspeed."

"Yeah," answered Lonan as he turned back up the ramp of the shuttle.

Telgrin watched his friends say their goodbyes. Then, out of the corner of his eye, he saw her. It was Sarah, the young medic that he could never seem to stop thinking about. She was an attractive woman in her late twenties. Her long, brown hair was always held up in a neat ponytail. Most days she wore her thin-rimmed glasses that Telgrin thought made her look not only extremely intelligent but also a hundred times more beautiful. At different times she was assigned to work with Averine in the med ward. On those days Telgrin always came up with some reason that he had to leave the shop or lab and take a message to Averine. The problem was that ninety-eight percent of the time he chickened out at the last second and ended up sheepishly dragging himself back to the shop only to be greeted by Lonan's annoying grin. Telgrin hated when he did that.

Sarah was walking across the hangar carrying medical supplies and heading for Sevran's shuttle. She must have somehow sensed that he was watching her, because she turned and looked back at him.

Telgrin quickly looked away and tried to appear to be doing something important and then ducked into the shuttle. Moments later the ramp pulled back into the hull of the ship and the door slowly closed and sealed.

Averine had slowly backed away from the shuttle and was standing in one of the doorways that led out of the hangar and back into the base. She stood and lovingly waved to Lonan as his head appeared in the cockpit window. He faked a smile and waved back as he thought of all that could happen here if he and the other teams failed in their rescue missions.

Telgrin sneaked a peek through one of the cockpit windows and watched Sarah as she walked back toward the outer edge of the hangar away from the engines and back to safety as they began to fire their warmup sequences.

He whispered to himself, "You could have a least waved."

"What was that?" asked Lonan.

"Nothing," shot back Telgrin, busying himself with work at his computer station behind the main pilot chairs.

Lonan smiled and shook his head a little as he saw Sarah walking though the hangar. "One of these days you're going to have to actually speak to her."

"I don't know who you're talking about," answered Telgrin without looking up from his computer terminals.

"We'll have to take care of that when we get back. For now, let's go save some slaves," said Lonan.

"Sounds good," answered Telgrin. He paused for a second and then quietly added, "I still don't know who you're talking about."

Lonan smiled and shook his head.

From high above on the balcony Kilgron looked down over the hangar and watched as hundreds of Helienders loaded into shuttles. He shifted painfully on his artificial leg as he watched his daughter saying goodbye to her husband. As a lifetime warrior it pained him to stay behind and to send his son-in-law into harm's way. He knew that his daughter, whom he loved more than life, would be devastated if anything were to happen to him.

All the shuttles had finished loading supplies and personnel. Most had already started their secondary engines and where nearly ready for takeoff. Sevran had just jumped into the co-pilot's chair and pulled on his helmet as his pilot fired up their warmup sequence.

Back in the valley that lay in front of the great gate, thousands of angels had gathered and still more continued to fly in. Some of them landed on cliffs on the side of the mountain up above the door. There they unpacked weapons from the side packs of their horses. As they assembled these it was clear that they were small catapults. Still more angels filled the valley below as Tekel, Balim, and Genon arrived on their horses.

They stood on a small ridge that ran out from the side of the mountain into the flat valley. From here they were elevated and could see the entire battlefield. They could also very plainly see the black storm clouds as they rolled across the valley. With their angelic eyes they could gaze far across the sky to see that in front of the clouds was a swarm of demons in flight. They were still many kilometers away but were moving very quickly. As they flew they seemed to pull the black clouds with them, their bodies erupting with lighting and thunder.

Tekel called his two generals to his side. "The humans will be leaving soon. I need you to take one warrior for each of their units and go to them now."

"Yes, sir," answered Balim and Genon. They rode down into the formations of the other angels to collect re-enforcements. As they did Tekel gazed off into the distance and watched the enemy draw near.

Meanwhile the Nemaron command ship hovered in the outer atmosphere of the largest planet in the Ruen star system. Ten other Nemaron carriers hovered in a defensive perimeter around the command ship. Ten fighters that had been patrolling flew in nearer to their carriers and landed in the hangars located on the sides of the enormous space craft.

On the command ship Maginon entered the main deck as a crew of thirty soldiers piloted the ship.

"Sir, all carriers have reported in and are ready to depart," the flight commander reported.

"Good. Get us clear of the meteor field and into formation," ordered Maginon. "I want all our forces to come out of light speed at the same time and in proper attack formation."

"Yes, sir."

All the Nemaron carriers flew through a dense pack of meteors that where stuck in orbit around the Ruen planet and out into a clearing in space at the outer ridge of the star system. Once the ten carriers had positioned themselves around the command ship, they held their positions and waited for orders from Maginon.

"All ships are in position, sir. We're ready to launch into lightspeed, waiting for your command," reported the flight commander.

Maginon could barely hear him as everything around him seemed to drift away. He closed his eyes and painfully slipped into a vision. He could hear a slight whisper that slowly grew in intensity. When he opened his eyes, he found himself standing in a strange, dark place. Wind circled him with enormous force, and he couldn't see where he was through a blurry mist. He could barely make out the sight of demons matching in the background as Satan stepped through the wind and into sight. In the background he could hear thunder and see lightning.

Then Satan spoke.

"I've given you a great many resources. Now you had better use them wisely."

"Yes, my lord," said Maginon as he bowed his head in fear as he tried to stand up against the winds.

"Begin the executions on time and stay on schedule. Do not fail me," said Satan as he stepped toward Maginon. The winds intensified, and Satan's voice rang in his ears until all was silent.

Maginon opened his eyes and found himself back on the command deck. He gasped for air as if waking from a nightmare.

"Sir, are you ok?" asked the flight commander.

"I'm fine. Have all slave camps report in."

As he said this a small amount of blood ran down from the corner of his eyes. He was visibly in pain as he sat down near the center of the command deck. He wiped his eyes, looked down at his hand, and found it covered in blood. He jumped back slightly and then looked around to see if anyone had seen him bleeding. He quickly wiped away all the blood and then sat back in the command chair.

Meanwhile, deep inside the mountain of the Helion base, Kilgron and many soldiers prepared for the Nemaron attack in the command center. One of the soldiers picked up a signal from his computer and reported to Kilgron. "Sir, the Nemaron ships have moved out of their cover and appear to be preparing to jump to light speed."

"How many?"

"We're getting a reading on eleven carriers in total, sir."

Kilgron turned to a nearby com link and called to the shuttles. From within the cock-pit of his ship Lonan heard him send the following message. "Launch all rescue shuttles now. Nemaron is on their way. All rescue shuttles launch immediately."

The three Seberian soldiers strapped into their seats. Lonan turned and asked, "Are you guys ready for this?"

"Are you?" answered one of the Seberians as Lonan peered out the cockpit window at his wife, who was still watching from the edge of the hangar.

"Yeah, let's go. We've got a job to do," answered Lonan. He gently eased up the engines, which lifted them a meter off the hangar floor and slowly hovered toward the door.

All the rest of the shuttles did the same as the engines created a deafening roar and powerful winds. One by one they worked their way out of the hangar and onto the launch pad on the side of the mountain base.

On the Nemaron command deck, Maginon regained his composure as he stood to listen as the slave camps reported in.

"Planet Warff reporting, we're on schedule and ready for execution, sir."

Then Devakin's voice came over the speaker. "Sir, planet Crule is ready for execution."

Maginon stepped to the computer in order to speak with Devakin. "Everything must go perfectly. You know the consequences of failure."

"Not to worry, sir. We've been looking forward to this. We're ready, and we have some additional help in case any problems should come up." As Devakin said this he looked out across the hundreds of slaves hanging above boiling pits of lava. Then what he was speaking of came into sight. Three demons flew across the room on their massive, bat-like wings as they patrolled the camp.

Maginon sat back down in the command chair and took a deep breath while trying not to draw attention to himself. "It's time. Launch all carriers on my mark. Now!"

Seconds later all eleven Nemaron carriers gradually accelerated and then all simultaneously fired secondary engines, sending them into light speed. Instantly they disappeared from the Ruen star system.

Chapter 4

At the great gate thousands of angels had gathered and filled the valley. Off in the distance the cloud of demons continued to draw near while three Leviathan soldier transports flew over the mountain range and headed toward the great gate.

"Let's give them a proper welcome," shouted Tekel to his angels gathered in the valley. As he said this he closed his eyes and began a low hum. The rest of the angels did the same. He then raised his hands with his palms facing the approaching enemy force. Moments later the branches of the trees behind them began to sway and the leaves turned upside down. A wind began to build, reaching intense force and speeds.

Everything in the valley swirled as Tekel and his angels stood with their hands raised and their voices joined in a deep low hum that had also grown in intensity with the wind. Then Tekel thrust his hands forward as if shoving something toward the enemy. With this the winds swept across the valley and collided with the demons and the storm clouds behind them. The massive force of wind sent them out of control. Most fell to the ground after colliding with each other. Some were slammed into the sides of the Leviathan transports, which spun out of control and fell out of the sky.

Inside the cockpits of the transports the pilots struggled to regain control. Finally they gave up and shouted to the men, "Evacuate!"

The soldiers jumped out of the open sides of the ship. Some of them survived the fall, but some did not. Seconds later the ships crashed to the ground in massive balls of flame. Alongside this the demons tried to collect themselves as the winds pinned them to the rocky terrain below.

Farther off in the distance Satan hovered above the mountain range as he rode is mutilated horse. He watched with no remorse as his forces were thrown to the ground. As the winds reached him he was forced to land. As the incredible force of the winds blew over him he hid himself under the protection of a large bolder. He clutched the stone to keep from being blown away.

In the sky above, the gusts of wind from the angels clashed with the storm clouds that Satan and his demons had created. Their black clouds soon dissipated and turned to thin wisps of grey mist. The lightning and thunder seemed to fight to remain as the last bit of thunder rolled across the valley. The two storms seemed to destroy each other as the winds died down and calm passed over the valley.

Satan jumped to the top of the boulder that he had been hiding under. He looked down to the valley below to find his three transports burning, many of his Leviathan soldiers lying dead and his demons struggling back to their feet. "I guess we'll march in," said Satan. He raised his right hand and gave out a deep, beast-like roar. Then, in the next valley behind him, an army of hundreds of thousands of Leviathan soldiers began to march forward. Over their heads flew another force of hundreds of demons. Satan smiled while he mounted his horse again as he watched his army on the march.

On planet Helion the six rescue shuttles blasted off from the launching rails and into the night sky. A fighter accompanied each one of them as they all flew toward the southern hemisphere of the planet. The Helion shuttles and fighters paired up and flew off in separate directions.

From the pilot's seat of his ship, Lonan called out to the rest of the Helion spacecraft. "Everyone get to your slave camps as quickly as possible and stay clear of any Nemaron ships. You can't fight them off and complete your missions at the same time. So move quickly and stay low."

"Roger that," each of the pilots radioed back.

Sevran switched on a com link that connected him directly to Lonan.

"Hey, be careful. Your wife will miss having you to boss around if you don't come back from this mission," said Sevran.

Lonan thought for a minute with an inquisitive look on his face. Then he grinned as he said, "You know, you're right. She would miss that. What does that say about us?"

"You're married."

"Take it easy, bachelorette."

"You take it easy. I'm just stating the facts."

"Yeah, well, you'll get there one day. Then you'll see what you've been missing," answered Lonan.

"Anyway, seriously. Be careful. You'll all I got—moron."

"Sad, right?" said Lonan with a smile.

"Tell me about it."

After seeing Cloin and Armon lose Ahren, they had a new appreciation for each other.

"These missions are crucial," said Lonan, his tone now far more serious. "If we fail, Helion is in trouble."

"Yeah. But we're on it. If you need me just call and I'll come bail you out," said Sevran with a grin.

"Ok. We need to cut the chatter. I'll see you back at base," answered Lonan.

"You got it, Sevran out."

In the valley in front of the great gate, the hundreds of thousands of Leviathan soldiers had reached the river that separated the valley. On the far side the angels and their horses covered the entire hill that led up to the large, wooden doors. They stood ready for battle without the slightest hint of fear.

As Satan's soldiers neared the river they formed ranks and stood at attention, awaiting their orders. The demons flew in and landed behind them. Some continued to fly as far as the river. They flew back and forth on their grotesque, batlike wings while they taunted and jeered the angels. Then Satan landed on a small hill in the center of his side of the valley. From there he could see all his soldiers and demons surrounding him on all sides. Abaddon and Abadile both flew in on the backs of their horrific horses and landed beside Satan. He turned to them and said, "Get those pigs into position."

"Yes, my lord," replied Abaddon. Then the two of them flew up and across the battlefield.

As they flew they roared out orders, which caused the commanders of the Leviathan to shout out more orders to their men. As this happened, the army of Leviathan spread out across the valley and widened their formations.

Satan flew up into the air and toward the great gate. As he did, Tekel flew up also, and they met in midair above the river.

"What are you doing here?" asked Tekel as he hovered on his horse. "Shouldn't you be hiding in your cave?"

"This is the great gate, isn't it?" asked Satan.

Tekel said nothing.

"Get out of my way. I'm taking this army through the portal. The throne of all creation will be mine. Move your army aside and I'll let you rule over the star systems. I *will* destroy Him and take over all worlds." Satan paused and enjoyed his own words for a moment then continued. "It would be wise of you to be on my good side."

"That sounds like the offer you gave the angels who were once under your command, and now they serve you like dogs." As Tekel said this he looked aside at Abaddon and Abadile. He thought back to the time before the war in heaven. With his mind's eye he remembered how noble, powerful, and perfect they once were. He was saddened to be reminded of what they had now become.

Tekel raised his voice. "Don't waste your words! You know we can't be corrupted. We'll stand in your way until the end of time when God himself will open all doors to the created world and unleash the rest of his army."

Satan squirmed in his saddle, his eyes burning with both hatred and fear.

"You know what will become of you then, don't you? They're not as patient as we are," said Tekel with a slight grin.

The army of angels that he was speaking of was primarily made up of Seraphim. They were larger and more powerful than most other angels. They also had four wings rather than two. All the angels had surrendered their free will to God so that they could not be corrupted by Satan, but they maintained their personalities. They were still independent beings. The Seraphim, however, were more aggressive and far less patient with humans and their willingness to cooperate with Satan.

God hated to do it, but He sometimes sent a pair of Seraphim to take care of particularly dangerous groups or situations. The Seraphim cared for humanity and even loved it just as God and the rest of the angels did. It was based on that love that they were more willing to destroy those who threatened the rest of creation. They were most protective of the weak or helpless. Their rage burned the most intensely for those who would harm or take advantage of children.

Satan's stomach turned as he thought of facing the Seraphim. He knew that they were waiting on the other side of the great gate, but he tried not to think of them. He and his demons had grown to be extremely powerful, but he still had some doubt about how and if they could defeat them.

The thought of failure roused Satan's rage, and he rose up in his saddle. "With the power that I now possess we will crush them also." His voice echoed as a multitude. Satan tried to regain his composure as he looked across the field of waiting warrior angels. "I hope you have more soldiers coming. Mine would at least like a challenge. Or is this all you have left? Have we killed the rest? Pity." Satan quickly turned and flew back to the mound in the center of his army.

Tekel stayed and hovered there for a while to look out across the massive army of Leviathan men. There were nearly five times as many men as the number of angels that he had assembled. He then turned and flew back down to his army below. He landed on the hill where two of his angels awaited him.

"He doesn't seem to know about the human counter attack. We must hold him here long enough for them to free the slaves," said Tekel.

"And keep him out of the great gate," added Balim.

"Yes. I think..." Tekel paused and looked out across Satan's army of men and demons. "This will be a long night."

Balim and Genon grunted in agreement.

Meanwhile, Sevran and his team decelerated out of light speed as they neared the planet Warff. It was still within the boundaries of galaxy 55x9 but on the opposite side of the center of the galaxy and far from the planet Helion. It was a barren planet on the surface, but the core was rich in precious minerals and elements that could be extracted from their raw materials. Nemaron had taken the planet captive and stripped it of nearly everything of value. Now the only thing that remained was a labyrinth of mines and a slave compound, which they were now ready to use to execute their captives.

Sevran's pilot landed two kilometers away from the compound while Sevran prepared his motorcycle and weapons. Through the clear night sky they could see the compound standing in the middle of an expansive flat land that extended for hundreds of miles. On the horizon they could make out only the slightest black rim of mountain ranges. The camp was very secluded. In a nearby hangar there sat only three Leviathan transport shuttles.

Inside the cargo bay Sevran finished his preparations as the shuttle touched down. The rest of his soldiers were also nearly ready to roll out; they mounted their motorcycles and strapped on their helmets. Sevran glanced around the cargo bay, checking on everyone's status, and saw the lone Seberian of the team.

The Seberian was still sitting on the far end of the cargo bay with his head down. Just then he slowly raised his head and opened his eyes. When he did, a white-hot light radiated from them and filled the end of the cargo bay. The light was so intense that Sevran winced a little when the Seberian turned and looked directly at him.

"Is everyone ready?" asked Sevran, to which all his soldiers answered in the affirmative. He asked everyone, but he was mainly wondering about the Seberian, who smiled and nodded.

"Praying?" asked Sevran.

"Yes," answered the Seberian; his eyes faded to the point that Sevran could look at him without pain.

"You ready?" asked Sevran.

"Very ready," answered the Seberian with another grin.

"Good." Sevran turned to address everyone. "We're the first team out. Let's show the rest of them how it's done."

The cargo bay door opened and the ramp extended out and down to the soft, sandy surface below. The soldiers fired up their engines and began to roll out. There were twenty of them in all including the Seberian, who had just thrown his leg over his motorcycle and strapped on his helmet. Very quickly and quietly they all rode off toward the compound.

Back at the great gate Satan landed on his command mound in the center of his army and gave out more orders. "Send in the pawns first. We'll let them tire the enemy for us."

"Yes, my lord," replied Abaddon. He turned and roared out orders in their grotesque demon tongue. This sent the first ranks of Leviathan soldiers on the march toward the river. These were all men filled with the supernatural evil power that Satan had placed in them. They were as strong as ten human men, and there was a force of hundreds of thousands of them just waiting for their time to fight.

The Leviathan soldiers advanced without question. They were not under some sort of a spell, nor were they possessed. They moved and acted of their own free will, but their minds were poisoned. Their eyes were darkened, clouded and filled with hate and greed. As they marched forward, they drew swords. They waded across the river that was only knee deep. Then, once on the other side, they began to run as they attacked the front lines of the angels.

As the Leviathan soldiers attacked, they divided into groups of five and converged on the angels five against one. The men were filled with so much of Satan's unholy power that they moved at speeds far faster than the human eye.

The angels drew their blades wreathed in lightning and battled the men in a blaze of sword play.

The Leviathan men surrounded them and attacked from all sides. The angels did the best that they could to not kill the men but to only beat them until they were knocked unconscious or bruised so badly that they were forced to pull out of the fight in order to recover.

Waves and waves of the Leviathan men passed over the river and crashed against the wall of angelic guardians.

Chapter 5

Meanwhile, back on the planet Warff, Sevran and his force entered the back side of the compound. They crept into the building and found their way to the main chamber.

Hundreds of slaves hung from their feet in the racks. Below them were wide open pits filled with a boiling black liquid. The smell of the building nearly made the men vomit.

One of the Helienders immediately launched four small sensors that hovered in place for moment then disappeared. They had turned on a cloaking hologram that hid them from the human eye. They then flew off in all directions and spread out around the compound to get readings.

"Have you located the control room?" asked Sevran, turning to the soldier who had just launched the drones.

The devices had just started to send back readings, which were then translated to digital 3-D holograms displayed on the top of his weapon. That hologram showed the entire building.

"Yeah, follow me. It's this way," answered the soldier.

Just then two Leviathan soldiers walked around the corner.

Sevran immediately fired two electric rounds and knocked the men out. They fell to the floor and shook from the electricity pulsating through them. Two Helienders stayed back to cover their exit while the rest of the team continued around the perimeter of the main chamber until they came to an elevated room that looked out over the slave racks.

Without a sound Sevran and his comrade climbed the stairs and entered the control room. Inside they found all the computer systems that were operating the entire compound and two Nemaron soldiers managing the computers.

One of the Helienders took out the two soldiers without them even knowing that they were there. Sevran and three of his soldiers then took over the room while the rest of the team stayed out of sight down in the main chamber. One of them immediately went to work and hacked into their system by connecting his own small computer. He then was quickly able to shut down the system. As he did, large platforms extended out from the floor and covered the oil pits below.

Then the racks began to lower.

"Ok, look out everybody. That's going to draw some attention," whispered Sevran into his com device. He exited the control room and walked down the stairs.

As the racks lowered the slaves began to come out of the tranced state. The rescue team ran to the captives and helped them as they struggled to free their feet from the rack system. Men, women, and children were all enslaved in this compound and had been only moments away from execution.

Just then fifteen Leviathan ran into the room and opened fire. Two Helienders where hit and killed instantly as rounds flew through their chests. The rest of the rescue team opened fire and took out the first eight Leviathan soldiers. The electric rounds traveled so fast and they were not able to dodge them. The other soldiers quickly noticed the advance in the new rounds and found a way to move even more quickly. Now that they could anticipate the speed of the rounds, they could dodge some of them.

The Leviathan soldiers then ran at a lightning speed as they attacked and killed four more of the Helion soldiers.

Suddenly the Seberian ran into the very center of the area that the seven remaining Leviathan soldiers were covering. As he did he pulled his blade and in a whirlwind of motion cut their rifles in half. Now with nothing to shoot they pulled their blades and engaged in sword battle. The Seberian could move so fast that his speed was equal to that of the Leviathan men. They could see each other's movements, but from the opposite side of the chamber the rest of the rescue team could see nothing but a dark blur of motion with the occasional spark from the clash of blades. He took on all seven of them at the same time. His focus and determination was perfect. They were powerful and fast, but also sloppy.

The rest of the rescue team wanted to help their team member, but they could barely see who was who, so they opened fire on the outer edges of the group. They managed to hit three Leviathan, which helped their Seberian friend tremendously.

As the men continued to fight, the effects of the drugs wore off on the slaves and they began to become aware of their surroundings again.

"What's going on?" asked one of the women.

"Don't worry, you're safe. We're here to rescue you," said Sevran as he helped her to her feet. "Come on, we need to get you out of here before reinforcements show up."

"Did you here that? We're free!" cried the woman to the man beside her.

The freed slaves all began to pass along the word that they had been recused as the Helienders helped them out of the racks.

Just then, a soldier of Helion ran over and reported to Sevran. "Other than these last few soldiers the chamber is secure and charges are set, but the shuttle sends word that men are on the way."

While he spoke the Seberian continued to hold the last three Leviathan soldiers at bay. As he fought he could see in the background that the red mist was dissipating. As the slaves were freed they no longer emitted the pain and suffering. The collection chamber's red light began to fade. Soon it was down to nearly nothing.

As this happened, the speed and strength of the Leviathan soldiers also faded. The loss in speed gave the Helienders a chance to pick off at least two more of them. This then allowed the Seberian to knock out the final soldier in just minutes.

The speed and intensity of the fight had taken a lot out of him. He took a minute and hunched over with his hands on his knees as he tried to catch his breath. He then looked over at Sevran who was helping a slave off the rack and gave him a tired thumbs up sign.

Sevran smiled back and then shouted out to the captives. "Ok, listen everyone. We're here to save you. Everybody stay close, stay quiet, and follow us to the shuttle."

As he said this the slaves followed them out of the building into the waiting shuttle. They stumbled as the effects of the drugs were still leaving their bodies.

Sevran and the Seberian were the last to leave the building, causally stepping around the bodies of the fallen Leviathan soldiers. They were not dead, but the electricity still pulsated through their bodies.

Before they left the main room, the Seberian looked up and saw that the collection chamber was dark and had shut down completely. Beside him he saw one of the explosive charges that the other soldiers had set. He picked it up and attached it to an arrow that he pulled from the quiver on his back. He then took his bow and fired the arrow into the ceiling directly beside the collection chamber. Then he ran from the building and into the shuttle as the last of the slaves were walking up the ramp.

Meanwhile, at the great gate the Leviathan soldiers were still attacking the angels. None of the angels had died, but they were all growing weary. They continued to fight as the piles of soldiers around their feet grew.

Then, suddenly, all of the Leviathan soldiers slowed simultaneously. They all felt a loss of power.

"*No!* Those fools." cried Satan, and his eyes burned with fury. "Something is wrong with the camps."

Back at the slave camp on planet Warff, Sevran and his crew had just started to take off in the main shuttle while their fighter escort was already in the air and preparing to exit the atmosphere.

"Ok, blow it," commanded Sevran from the pilot seat of his shuttle.

The co-pilot hit some buttons on the control panel. This triggered the detonation count down on the charges that they had left all throughout the slave compound. Just as they reached a distance of one kilometer, the charges exploded. As they did they destroyed all the computer systems and the hanging racks.

The collection chamber was also completely destroyed as the charge beside it exploded. A small blast came from each door and window of the compound, and black smoke surrounded the building.

"I guess they won't be using that camp again," said Sevran, smiling as he flew the ship out of the planet's atmosphere.

At the great gate the Leviathan soldiers continued their attempt to overpower the angels. From above on the mountain side the angels fired their catapults. Each of them launched a massive bundle that rolled through the air like a cannon ball. Just before they hit the ground they unfolded and spread out into heavy metal nets. These landed on large numbers of Leviathan soldiers. Then the angels pointed their blades at the nets and sent lightning bolts and electricity flowing through them, which knocked out all the Leviathan at the same time.

Then several angels flew down and picked up the nets full of unconscious soldiers. Each net carried seventy-five to eighty men. They flew them off the battlefield and laid them far to the side.

"Get those fools out of our way," commanded Tekel. "They've no idea how lucky they are that we're this patient with them."

"Stupid, weak humans," cried Satan. "First battalion, attack!"

With this, a third of the demons flew up into the sky and over the human soldiers. While in midair the flames of their blades grew in intensity. They fired balls of fire from the tips of their swords.

The angels pulled out their shields to protect themselves. Many of the balls of fire missed the angels and hit the Leviathan soldiers. This burned them to the bone in seconds and killed many of them. The demons then landed in the clearing below and engaged the angels in sword battle. The demons seemed to have a slight speed and strength advantage. The human soldiers also continued to attack the angels who had to now defend against both attackers.

At the home base on Helion the last rays of light disappeared from the dim, starlit sky as men, women, and children ran into one of the hangar doors. Cloin and other soldiers stood outside the door and directed them where to go.

"This way—come on—quickly," said Cloin as she pointed into the hangar.

Just at that moment Averine arrived in a Jeep. She stepped out and said to Cloin, "This should be everyone. These are the last of the outlanders." She could see that Cloin's attention was stolen as she gazed up into the sky. Averine turned to see eleven Nemaron carriers surrounded by hundreds of fighters entering Helion's distant outer atmosphere.

"Well, we're right on time. They're here," said Cloin.

Averine tried not to show the fear that seized her. The size of the approaching army sent a chill up her spine. "Get them into the bunkers now!" she shouted to the soldiers.

"That's everyone," she said into the com device on her wrist as she turned and entered the base. "Shut all doors and secure all hangars."

Coin gazed up at the ships as her eyes began to glow and intensify to a burning, white-hot light.

Chapter 6

The second Heliender team had landed on the planet Larm in galaxy 55x8. It was a very warm planet that was full of life and heavy vegetation. The team of seven Helienders and one Seberian crept their way through thick ground cover as they used their night vision equipment to navigate through the deep-black night of the jungle.

Finally they reached a clearing and found the Nemaron compound nestled at the bottom of an enormous mountain range. The mountains up above were covered in trees that reached heights of nearly ninety meters.

A rushing river moved down the side of the mountain and formed a thirty meter tall waterfall that sent mist into the air throughout the entire clearing. The compound was a large, three-story metal building that was covered in moss and rust from the massive amounts of moisture in the air.

The team crouched on the edge of the jungle hiding in the cover of the thick vegetation. Unnoticed by the team, a three-meter-long snake slowly crept down from a branch above and very carefully coiled itself about the upper body of one the Helion soldiers. He didn't see anything until it had completely wrapped around his body twice and its head was nearing his waist.

When he finally felt it he jumped backward and frantically struggled to pull it off his body. Because they were tactical, he didn't scream out and tried to stay quiet to prevent giving away their position to any Nemaron or Leviathan soldiers that could be nearby on patrol.

When the other soldiers saw what was happening, they pulled back away from the snake and took aim with their rifles. They knew they couldn't fire, but the natural response was to point their weapons at a threat.

The Heliender struggled to free himself and to find the head as he knew that there must be fangs somewhere around his body. The snake began to tighten its grip as the other soldiers found and grabbed hold of the tail of the creature. It was a large and powerful reptile. Its body was nearly one third of a meter in circumference in its largest part. The other soldiers worked to pin it down in order to gain control of it, but it was very strong and it took three men to pin its tail to the ground.

The solider frantically flipped over and over, trying to maintain his breath while fighting against the power of the creature until he finally found its head. This was a strange species that none of them had ever seen before.

As the serpent pinned the soldier to the ground, it slowly raised its hideous head and prepared to take a deadly strike. It had four large yellow eyes above its enormous mouth that stretched all the way across its head, which was nearly twice the size of that of the soldier. The animal slowly pulled its head back and opened its mouth to reveal eight very long fangs, four on the top and four on the bottom. The top ones started to secrete venom that dripped down onto the soldier's chest, when suddenly a blade flew through the serpent's neck.

It stood perfectly still for a moment, and then its head slowly rolled off its body, which started to twitch and slowly fell to the ground.

The dead body loosened its grip, and the soldier worked frantically to free himself. Once free he looked up to see the Seberian kneeling beside him with his sword still extended out over the body of the enormous snake.

"Thanks," said the soldier, attempting to regain his breath.

The Seberian nodded and smiled. He put his blade back in its sheath on his back and then offered the solider his hand. The Heliender took his hand and was lifted from the ground.

"Ready?" asked the Seberian.

"Yeah."

The rest of the soldiers threw the snake body to the side and pulled their attention back to the compound that sat on the other side of the fifteen-meter wide river moving swiftly in front of them.

The Seberian turned to the rest of the soldiers. "If this planet has these kinds of snakes in its jungles, I hate to see what is in that water."

"Agreed," said the Helion unit commander. "Set up the rope bridge."

Instantly three Helienders went to work on the bridge. The first pulled a modified crossbow from his pack. He loaded it with a thick, shafted arrow and shot it across the river and through small tree on the other side. As the arrow penetrated the tree the point protruded from the far side. When it did the tip expanded and folded out metal brackets that prevented it from pulling back through the hole in the tree. The tail of the arrow was attached to a spool of cable on the end to the crossbow.

The other two soldiers took the cable and attached it to a tree behind them, being very careful to not rouse any more snakes or other creatures. Once it was tightly secured, the first soldier attached a small device to the cable. It had six wheels and an electric motor. He locked it onto the cable and then attached a strap from his harness to it. Now that he was attached, he leaned back and put all his weight onto it. The cable was so tight that it easily kept him two meters off the ground. Once horizontal he triggered the motor, and it carried him across the river in seconds. After he reached the other side, he better secured the arrow and cable.

Within minutes the rest of the team did the same, and all reached the compound side of the river. There wasn't much vegetation cover, so they all stayed very low as they made their way to the nearest wall of the building. On the backside of the compound they found one lone door that didn't have any security or sensors attached.

As they passed through the door they found themselves in the corner of the main chamber. Thousands of people hung on a wooden rack system suspended above large metal vats of boiling water. The chamber was filled with smoke from the fires that raged underneath the vats that were suspended one meter above the floor.

As the Seberian surveyed the room he could see the red mist that was being emitted from the slave's bodies. It blended with the smoke from the fires as it poured from their bodies.

On the wall there was a clock that read four minutes fifty seconds and was counting down. The unit commander saw it and whispered, "Let's move, we don't have much time."

As they made their way across the room toward the command center on the far side, two Leviathan soldiers walked in while on patrol. The Helienders shot them with the electric rounds, and the Leviathan hit the floor unconscious.

Just then four more entered and found them on the floor.

"Intruders!" they yelled.

Seconds later the alarm system in the base sounded.

The Seberian stepped up and took out one of the Leviathan soldiers with another electric round. He then charged the other three and engaged them in hand-to-hand combat. His eyes blazed with intense white light as he defeated the first of the three. He and the other two remaining Leviathan engaged in ultra-fast combat that could barely be seen by the Helienders.

Three more Leviathan soldiers poured into the room. They immediately fired on the Heliender team making their way to the command center. Two of the men were shot and killed instantly while the rest tried to take cover.

"You two, come with me!" yelled the Helion commander. They jumped out from behind cover and ran toward the command center while returning fire on the Leviathan. The rest of the team stayed in their positions and provided cover fire.

The three reached the command center and kicked down the door to find two Nemaron soldiers running the execution racks. They immediately were knocked out with the electric rounds. As they lay on the floor twitching the commander reached for the control panel to shut down the execution. The countdown on the computer matched the one on the wall, which was now down to two minutes thirty seconds.

Just before he could reach the control panel another Leviathan soldier jumped through the glass enclosure and knocked him to the ground. The two Helienders opened fire, but the Leviathan had become aware of the new weapon they were using. He dodged all the rounds as he flipped backward. He grabbed a scrap piece of metal lying on the floor and used it as a shield to deflect the rest of the rounds. This allowed him to creep closely enough to grab the two Helienders. He ripped their weapons from their hands and picked them up off the floor by their throats, one in each hand.

Down below in the chamber the Seberian had just finished defeating the three Leviathan soldiers. As he stood and tried to catch his breath he looked up into the control room to see the men getting choked. He took careful aim with his rifle and fired three rounds at the enemy soldier.

Without even seeing the rounds coming the Leviathan soldier jumped backward to avoid all three. It was as if he could sense them coming. This caused him to lose his grip on the two men, who fell to the ground clutching their throats as they tried to breathe again.

Meanwhile, outside of the camp, an angel flew through a portal that opened for a split moment in the night sky. He rocketed toward the compound, but just before he reached the building a demon materialized to the side of the angel. The demon flew in and attacked in midair; tackling the angel to the ground.

As they both jumped to their feet, they drew swords and immediately went into battle. Their blades rang out as the lightning of the angels sword blended with the red-orange fire of the demons. The battle went on for too long until the angel was able to strike such a massive blow that the demon was sent sailing backward, writhing in pain. As the demon lay on the ground, cursing with black blood squirting from his arm, the angle was able to quickly escape and continued on his way toward the compound.

"Where are you going?" The demon laughed as the wound on his arm healed and stopped bleeding. He then jumped into the air and took to flight.

The angel was only fifty meters away from entering the compound when another demon appeared, stepping through another portal. He pulled his blade from the sheath on his hip, and it ignited with red flame. The demon pointed the sword tip at the angel and sent numerous balls on fire flying through the hot night air. The angel saw them coming just in time to raise his shield and block them. Fire and ash fell everywhere. Some of it hit the angel's legs and burned deep into his skin. He cried out in pain as the demon flew down into his path and hovered between him and the compound.

The other demon then flew in behind him and the two began to circle. The angel collected himself, trying to ignore the pain. As he prepared himself for the two on one battle he thought, "I don't have time for this. I must get inside."

Inside the compound the countdown had reached two minutes. When that happened, the racks automatically began the lowering procedure. As they began to lower, the jarring movement brought the slaves out of their comatose haze. They could now see that they were being lowered headfirst into boiling vats of water. They cried out in terror as they squirmed and tried to free themselves from the shackles of the racks.

The Seberian ran and jumped with supernatural speed and strength through the broken window of the command center. He landed just behind the Leviathan soldier and quickly took out his legs with a sweeping kick. That gave the Helienders just enough time to get through to the control panel as they scrambled to shut down the execution.

"Hurry up!" yelled one the soldiers; he looked out to see the slaves only two meters away from the tops of the vats. He also saw his fellow Helion soldiers finally overpowered by the Leviathan. They pulled the soldiers from the places where they had been taking cover. The Leviathan effortlessly threw them across the room and beat them until they were unconscious. The Leviathan then took the Helienders and tossed their unconscious bodies into the vats of boiling water.

The Seberian could sense the murder that had just taken place. With one powerful movement he reached down and ripped the amulet from the chest of the Leviathan that he was fighting.

The unholy power immediately left his body as he lay on the floor crying out in pain. The Seberian turned to see an immense amount of red mist pour out of the vats where the Helienders had just died. He alone could see it, and it was a sobering reminder of what would happen to the slaves if they were not successful in this mission.

The Leviathan soldiers in the chamber down below now turned their attention to the control room and began to make their way across the room. At the same moment three more Leviathan poured into the command center.

"Pull the bypass release lever," one yelled to the others.

The Seberian ran across the room at lightning speed and intercepted two of the Leviathan as they tried to pull the manual release. They all pulled blades and engaged in a two versus one sword battle. While they were locked in a blazing-fast hand-to-hand battle, the two Helienders tried to hack the system and shut down the lowering mechanism. The third Leviathan, however, jumped over all the others and landed in the back corner of the room directly in front of the long, rusty release lever.

The Seberian watched from the corner of his eye as the Leviathan grabbed hold to the lever and began to pull down.

Suddenly a singing of a flying metal object flew past and a heavenly blade imbedded itself in the wall beside the lever. The Leviathan looked down to find that the flying blade had cut off both his arms before he was able to pull the lever. Once the momentary shock wore off he fell backward and screamed in pain.

Out in the main chamber the angel flew through the air with the two demons close behind. They weaved in between the upper portions of the slave racks as the demons sent balls of fire from the ends of their blades, each one just barely missing the angel.

As the hand-to-hand combat continued inside the command center, one of the Leviathan landed a massive punch to the Seberian's face, which sent him flying backward and slamming into the control panel. That gave the Leviathan a split second to get away and grab the lever.

As the angel flew through, dodging deadly fire from the demons, he raised his bow and pulled back an arrow. Just then one of the demons caught him by the boot, pulled him back, and slammed him against the wall. Pieces of wood and portions of the wall went flying in every direction from the impact the angel's body.

The demon ripped the bow from his hands and released an incredible barrage of punches that the angel frantically worked to block.

Inside the command center the Leviathan soldier pulled the lever and the racks were let free. The slaves and the racks began to free fall. The angel broke free from the demon's blade attack and grabbed hold of two of the nearest slave racks. Each one held thirty people. He struggled to lift them as the slaves inside where only centimeters from being immersed in the boiling water.

The other racks fell into the vats. The slaves screamed in anguish, but their voices were quickly drowned as their heads hit the water.

"NO!" cried the angel, as he could only watch them die.

As they did the red mist completely filled the room. The collection chamber pulsated with power and lit up the ceiling.

As the demons drew near, the angel grabbed two cables from each of the racks that he was holding and tied them together. He then carried them all in his left hand, pulling a second sword from its sheath with his right. His powerful wings beat with tremendous force as he tried to lift them higher above the vats. His eyes burned with white light as the demons attacked in from opposite sides. The white of his eyes intensified as the battle continued and he held off the attacks of both demons.

The remaining Helion soldiers looked on in heartache and fear. The Leviathan soldiers grabbed them and threw them through the window of the command center and onto the main chamber below. All the Helienders grouped together as the Leviathan slowly gathered around them.

"Now it's your turn," sneered one of the soldiers as they closed in.

The Seberian continued to battle one particularly powerful Leviathan back in the command center. When the execution happened the Seberian could not only sense but also see the Leviathan's speed and power increase.

In the midst of battle the Seberian closed his eyes while continuing to defend against each blade swing of the Leviathan. With eyes closed he called out to God for help. When he reopened his eyes the light blazed even brighter, his strength increased, and he pushed back the Leviathan.

With a strike so fast that the enemy couldn't even see it the Seberian ripped the amulet from his chest. The Leviathan dropped to his knees as he cried out it pain, but before his knees could touch the ground the Seberian had jumped through the window and landed beside the Helienders. He pulled a second blade from its sheath and took a defensive stance as the Leviathan slowly closed in on the Helion force.

The angel began to lose his grip as he still held sixty of the slaves from falling to their deaths. The demons continued to attack him from both sides, but he amazingly was able to defend each sword strike. The demons enjoyed the red mist as it poured into the demons bodies. The angel could see that their speed and power increased as the mist continued to fill the main chamber.

Chapter 7

A t the portal the angels were still locked in battle with both the Leviathan soldiers and demons. Satan and all his soldiers received a boost of power from the execution on the planet Larm; the red mist welled up inside them and poured from their eyes, ears, and mouths. This gave them a definite speed and power advantage. The Leviathan soldiers attacked with even more boldness and power. That distracted the angels long enough that the demons were able to give some deadly blows. A few of the angels were lost as some were stabbed through the heart while others had their heads removed by flaming demon blades. They could heal from all other types of wounds, but these two were deadly.

Back on planet Larm the Helion soldiers gathered what weapons they could find as the Leviathan closed in.

The demons continued to attack the angel with increased speed and power until one of them cut the inside of his left arm very deeply. That caused him to lose his grip on the cables. Seconds later the slaves cried out in anguish as they hit the boiling water. In seconds their cries were gone, but they were replaced by the roars of the two demons and the Leviathan soldiers.

"No!" cried out the Helienders, hope draining from their faces.

The Seberian used the fact that his enemy was distracted by celebration and knocked four of the Leviathan unconscious when he shot them with Lonan's electric rounds. That pulled the Helion soldiers back to reality and gave them a chance to escape.

"That door over there," yelled the Helion commander, pointing to a door at the end of a hallway on the outer edge of the main chamber. The remaining seven Helienders opened fire with electric rounds as they ran for the door. They hit just a few of the Leviathan as they ran toward the exit. The rest dodged the rounds and ran in pursuit.

As the Seberian also ran toward the door he grabbed one of the Helion backpacks and opened it up. Inside was an explosive charge. As he ran he started the timer. Two Leviathan where catching up to him and about to catch him when two electric rounds that where shot from the far side of the room took them out. The Helion soldiers were providing cover fire from the door as the team tried to evacuate.

As the Seberian ran toward the door he looked up at the angel still working desperately to fight off the two demon attackers. They swirled through the air like tornados. The Seberian passed underneath them, and they locked eyes. His look seemed to ask, "What can I do?"

The angel yelled down, "Go! I will hold them off."

Then something happened that no one had anticipated: The Leviathan soldiers that had been shot with the electric rounds began to wake up far sooner than had been calculated. The concentration of the red mist and its power had shortened the length of time that the rounds had an effect on their bodies.

As they left the building, the Helienders also set charges that they pulled from their backpacks. They threw them into a side room that was filled with advanced electronic equipment.

When they all exited the building, they found their shuttle waiting just outside the door and their fighter escort hovering up above. The Seberian was the last to jump through the shuttle door as the main engines fired and they lifted away from the building.

Just as they began to fly away from the compound the angel was overpowered and thrown to the floor. They pinned him down as one of the demons raised his flaming blade to strike a deadly blow. Just then the main chamber was filled with flames as all the charges exploded.

As the shuttle flew away, the Helienders could see Leviathan soldiers running from the building, flames engulfing the compound.

Back at the portal to heaven the angels and demons continued in their battle while the demons had a definite advantage. The Leviathan soldiers that had been knocked out by the electric nets were now awake and rejoined the fight.

"We need to give the men more time. I think it's time for re-enforcements," said Tekel as he flew to the small clearing in front of the door in the mountain. He thrust his sword into the ground and knelt beside it. He extended his arms out to his sides and then with tremendous force clapped his hands together against the flat sides of his blade. He did that three times, and each time the blade acted like a tuning fork and sent shockwaves through ground.

Moments later the side of the mountain in front of him started to shake and crumble. All the dirt on each side of the door crumbled as two massive angels immerged from under the mountain. They stood seven meters tall and were made completely of stone. They shook themselves off and stretched as if they had been sleeping for hundreds of years. God had stationed these angels here as guardians of the great gate. They had been buried to stay hidden and to not draw attention to the door.

"I'm sorry to awaken you, my brothers, but we need your help," said Tekel as he flew up into the air to speak with them. "As you can see, the fallen one and his minions are trying to pass through the gate."

The angels nodded their heads and shook all the rubble from their bodies. They extended their massive stone wings and pulled their swords from their sheaths. Their blades and their eyes both lit up with blinding-white light. Electric current pulsated over the surface of their blades. They each gave out a roar that echoed across the planet.

"We are ready," they said in deep, echoing voices.

Tekel flew up into the air above the battlefield and yelled in an unusually loud voice: "Everyone stop, NOW!"

As he said this he plummeted downward and punched the ground. The impact was so great that it created a violent earthquake. All the Leviathan fell to the ground and the angels and demons fought to regain their footing. He then flew back up into the air to address the battlefield.

"Men of creation, hear me now! Until this point we have shown you mercy, but no more! If you do not abandon this attack and march off this battlefield, you will die. I know you can hear and understand me. The enemy has not taken control of you fully. You have been warned, and you are responsible for your own actions. Whatever he has promised you is a lie. He is only using you for his own evil purposes. You have the choice to walk away from this evil path now. If you do not, you will perish. The choice is yours."

Satan flew up into the air and hovered above the Leviathan on his side of the battle field. "Don't listen to this fool. Beyond that door lies power, riches, and glory. Follow me and we will take it by force."

All the human Leviathan stood to their feet and cheered. They picked up their weapons and charged the angels once again.

The angels' eyes all burned in unison with the same intensity. As the wave of Leviathan soldiers hit their ranks, they did not hold back. They killed each of the men that attacked them quickly and with great ease. The demons then also rejoined the fight. They were still filled with great speed as the red mist continued to well up inside them.

The stone angels raised their swords and pointed them at Satan's forces. They released massive bolts of lightning from the tips of their blades, which took out hundreds of demons and Leviathan soldiers at one time.

Chapter 8

Maginon stood in the center of the command bridge as his soldiers operated the ship from their workstations.

"Sir, we're nearing the planet Helion and starting our deceleration out of light speed," reported the fight commander.

Moments later all the Nemaron carriers slowed and came out of light speed. As they did, the planet Helion came into sight. Maginon looked out the window and gazed at the planet with a lustful grin. His ten invasion carriers remained in defensive positions on all sides of the command ship as they continued to draw nearer the planet Helion.

"Launch long ranger fighters," ordered Maginon.

"Yes, sir."

In the hangars of all the Nemaron carriers, Leviathan soldiers marched in formation as they loaded onto the troop transport shuttles. In other hangars the fighter shuttles finished loading fuel and fired their secondary engines, which gently lifted them from the deck of the hangar and into a hover mode.

Inside the cockpit of the fighters the Nemaron pilots strapped themselves in as they received a transmission from the command ship.

"First wave long range fighters launch immediately. Repeat, first wave fighters clear for launch."

Within seconds twenty heavily armed Nemaron fighters launched from each of the carriers. Once clear of the larger ships they fired their main engines and rockets toward the planet Helion.

On the command bridge Maginon watched as his fighters spread out across the surface of the planet and created a defense grid to prevent any Helienders from escaping.

"As soon as they are in range, fire the catalyst missiles," ordered Maginon.

"Yes, sir," replied one of his soldiers.

Moments later catalyst missiles launched from tubes on the front of the command ships. Each ship fired two missiles that sped directly toward the base under the mountain. They spread out evenly as they passed through the atmosphere. The Nemaron fighters had stopped and were hovering just outside the outer atmospheric layer. They watched as the catalyst missile raced toward the Helion stronghold. Once the missiles had reached the base, they stopped and hovered one hundred meters above the surface of the planet.

From the outside, the mountain looked completely uninhabited. All hangar doors and hatches were closed and covered with cloaking holograms. But deep inside the mountain all the people of Helion barricaded themselves in their bunkers.

In the war room Averine, Kilgron, and Cloin watched on large monitors the Nemaron command ships drawing closer. They could see the catalyst missiles as they came to a stop and hovered far above the base.

"Sir, their catalyst missiles have entered our atmosphere," reported one of the woman Helion soldiers.

"Send out a warning," replied Kilgron.

All throughout the base the people heard the warning. "Attention, prepare for impact. Repeat, everyone prepare for impact."

On the bridge of the Nemaron command ship Maginon grinned as their craft drew closer to the planet's surface. "Activate catalysts," he ordered.

"Yes, sir."

Moments later all twenty of the missiles exploded simultaneously. The explosions were not very large, but the shockwaves were. The entire mountain shook as if a tremor had crept from the depths of the planet. The hydro-cells buried deep in the center of the mountain continued on without any problem.

Everyone inside the mountain base shook and struggled to maintain their footing. The lights went off and on for a few seconds and then everything settled and returned to normal.

"We'd better get down to the hangar," said Averine. She turned and walked toward the door, Cloin following her.

"Averine. Be careful," said Kilgron. It pained him to see her go. He wished there was some way that he could keep her out of the battle and inside the base.

She stopped and turned back to face her father. She smiled as she replied, "Yes, sir."

He forced a smile and then tried to clear his head as he turned his attention back to the monitors in the command center. "Launch air defense. Send up the fighters," he ordered.

On the surface of the mountain large, tubular ports emerged from under a thin layer of dirt and twigs. They extended out from the center of the mountain until they were several meters above the ground. The mouth of the tubes opened to reveal the oscillating lights moving up the inner surface of the launch tube.

Inside the mountain pilots continued loading into the cockpits of their fighters, which were then mechanically loaded onto a conveyer that rolled toward the inside end of the launch tubes.

One after another they were moved into position at the bottom of the tube and then magnetically pulled through to the top. As they neared the outer end of the tube they picked up speed until they were fired from the surface of the mountain.

From outside hundreds of fighters could be seen as they launched in many different directions. Each squadron then regrouped and flew in defensive formations far above the mountain as they raced out to meet the oncoming Nemaron air attack.

In the control room of the main command ship Maginon jumped to his feet, amazed to see the Helion fighters as they flew from the mountain and turned toward his ships.

"Sir, it appears that the catalyst missiles had no effect," sheepishly reported one of his soldiers.

"I see that, you idiot! They must use some alternative power system. Fire all missiles!" cried Maginon.

The Nemaron carriers launched another batch. These were not catalysts but very destructive air-to-surface missiles. They raced through the air toward the base. The Helion fighters broke formation and made space as they passed by in the opposite direction.

The Helion squadron leader called back to the base, "Missiles on the way."

"Roger that, we see them," the command center responded.

"Launch countermeasure missiles," commanded Kilgron. Seconds later hidden rocket launchers appeared from under the ground all across the surface of the mountain. Each of them fired numerous missiles, which immediately began to track and seek out the incoming Nemaron ammunition. Once the Helion countermeasures had found their target, they split open and attached themselves to the shaft of the Nemaron missiles. They transformed into what looked like a collar, which then projected a spherical force field around itself and the Nemaron ammunition to which it was attached.

With the outer sphere in place, the Helion counter measures then detonated, causing the Nemaron missile to also explode. As they did the entire explosion was contained within the spherical shield, which then fell to the ground and gradually rolled to a stop. The spheres steamed as the chemical reaction from the catalyst neutralized and absorbed all the energy from the explosion. Everything inside the sphere then condensed into stable elements.

Maginon jumped to his feet again as he watched his missiles neutralized. "*What was that?*" he yelled, and his soldiers cringed.

No one answered.

"Launch all fighters and ground assault transports, *now!*" His nostrils flared, and his eyes began to burn with a red haze.

Massive hangar doors slid back on the tops of the Nemaron carriers. Seconds later hundreds of Nemaron fighters took off from these hangars, as did large, heavily armed transport ships. The transports turned and flew toward the planet while the fighters headed toward the Helion spacecraft that had nearly reached them.

The Helion fighter squad leader called out to his other fighters. "Second and third squads target the guns on the carriers. Fourth and fifth squads, you've got the fighters. Everyone else follow me. We've got to stop those transports before they get to the planet. Remember, we're using disabling missiles. The goal is to leave them floating in space, not dead."

"That's ridiculous. They're trying to kill us," answered one of the fighter pilots as several Nemaron rounds bounced off his forward shields.

"Don't argue. You heard the briefing. The more killing that happens just gives these freaks more power. So stick to the mission," ordered the squad leader.

More Helion fighters launched from the base and turned to join the huge space dog fight that was happening all around the Nemaron carriers. Guns mounted on the side of the ships unleashed wave after wave of rounds and destroyed many of the Helion fighters. Nearly half the Helion force split off and hunted down the transports heading toward the planet. They fired their specialized missiles, which hit the transports shields. When they did electrical current danced across the shield but did not penetrate or shut them down.

"Sir, we can't get through their shields," reported one of the Helion pilots as he pulled away from just attacking the transport nearest the planet.

"I see that. Let's hit them with multiple missiles at the same time. That should overload their shields and shut them down," answered the squad leader.

Three Helion fighters converged on one of the Nemaron transports. As they approached they fought their way through enemy fighters that were covering the Nemaron ships. They each fired three missiles and hit the target at nearly the same time. That sent a massive amount of power surging over the shields and down into the ship.

Seconds later the shields dissolved as the current dissipated.

"Shields are down, hit it!" shouted the squad leader. They each fired another missile, which all passed directly through and hit the hull of the Nemaron transport. The current penetrated all areas of the ship until the engines flickered and finally shut down.

Inside, the Leviathan crew scrambled to try to get the engines back on. While they did, current passed all over the control panel and inside hull of the spacecraft.

Back inside the Helion hangar the doors were still shut; soldiers scrambled to finish loading ammunition and weapons into the AUVs and Stingers. Averine and Cloin watched the air battle going on from monitors in the AUVs and could see some of the transport ships getting passed the Helion fighters.

"They need to take out more of those transports or else we'll have a too many Leviathan soldiers on our hands," said Cloin.

"Don't worry. They'll shut more down," replied Averine. As she turned to walk away, she struggled to convince herself.

On a distant desert planet in galaxy 55x8 Armon landed his shuttle in an open, sand-covered valley. The planet was small and barren. Its two suns made its climate extremely hot during the day and not much cooler during the night, which only lasted three hours. This was the home base of the Seberians who were given the responsibility to take care of this galaxy.

As Armon stepped off his shuttle he walked toward the base of a rock-covered ridge. Buried deep between two enormous boulders was a small cave. As Armon walked toward it the wind picked up and set sand flying in all directions. The wind and sand was so heavy that he couldn't see anything. He stopped walking and just covered his face. After a few seconds the sand storm died down and he was able to open his eyes.

When he did, he found three men standing directly in front of him. They were dressed in light-tan battle uniforms with military-grade armor. Their faces and eyes where completely covered with not only helmets and goggles but also air filtration masks. They were each armed with pistols on their thighs as well as swords attached to their backs.

"It's been a lot time, my friend," said the man standing in middle as he stepped forward. He paused for a moment then grabbed Armon and hugged him with bear-like force.

"Yes, it has." Armon struggled to regain his breath.

The man released him and said, "Come inside and get out of the sand and sun. I wouldn't want you to melt. Our planet is far different than the ice cube you call a home."

"Yes, please," said Armon; he smiled and followed the three men back to the cave. They walked through several meters of dark rock cave until they came to a metal door. They entered through it and then wound their way down a long staircase.

After a few more minutes of winding through the entrance to their base Armon found himself deep underground, sitting in the command center of a fellow group of Seberians. Their leader was an old friend of Armon and had been one of the first Seberians he had come to know.

His name was Eliune. He was a very large and muscular man. He stood well over two meters tall and could easily intimidate most people he met, whether he wanted to or not. His stature was intimidating, but his face was not. He had bright energetic eyes that always looked cheerful. His smile put everyone at ease, which was good because his size did not.

Armon filled him in on everything that was happening.

"I'm sorry that I don't have more time to catch up, but the enemy is on the way and time is short," said Armon.

"Think nothing of it," answered Eliune. "We're ready when you are. We're thirty Seberians strong and growing, and we would be honored to fight alongside you."

"Thank you, my friend. I'll be waiting in my shuttle."

"We'll meet you in the air," said Eliune with a wide smile.

Just moments later Armon lifted his shuttle up off the ground and prepared to take off from the planet. As he finalized launch preparations, he looked thought the cockpit canopy to find the desert floor opening. Seconds later Eliunes shuttle lifted up out of a hidden hangar underneath the desert floor. Once the shuttle cleared the opening the hangar hatch immediately closed again and sand rolled across it to conceal its location.

"Lead the way, Armon," radioed Eliune from the cockpit of his shuttle.

Armon fired his main engines, as did Elinue's pilot, and both Seberian shuttles raced toward space on their way back to the planet Helion.

Chapter 9

Meanwhile, Lonan piloted his shuttle as they neared their destination. Through the glass of the cock-pit a small planet could be seen coming into view. Beside him sat a co-pilot and behind him Telgrin worked at a computer station.

Lonan turned to him. "Begin scanning the building and find the main control room."

"I'm already on it," answered Telgrin.

"Here, take the controls," said Lonan to his co-pilot.

"Yes, sir," he replied.

Lonan got out of his seat and stood behind Telgrin and watched over his shoulder. On the workstation panel was a 3-D image of the compound. They could see through the building as the computer analyzed every detail. Just then one of the Seberians entered the cockpit.

"I've found the command center," said Telgrin. He zoomed in and through the holographic image of the Nemaron building. "But the computer is showing almost five thousand people being held in the racks."

"What?" responded Lonan.

"We can't carry that many," said Telgrin.

"We'll have to improvise. Send word to the base. Maybe they can get another transport on the way," ordered Lonan.

The Seberian interjected, "With that many people there's no doubt that this is where he's gathering a large amount his power."

"That just makes this mission that much more important. Let's go." Lonan walked out of the cockpit.

In the cargo bay ten Helion soldiers and two Seberians had just finished putting on jumpsuits and packing their gear as Lonan walked in. The men circled around for a quick briefing as Lonan stepped into the middle. Just as he started to speak Telgrin also walked in to put on his jumpsuit.

"We just found out that this camp is bigger than we thought. There are five thousand slaves being tortured in that building. This is where the enemy is getting most of his power. We must free those people. Remember, 'Save the slaves, save our planet.' Everyone back home is depending on us." Lonan scanned their faces and could see the apprehension. Except for the Seberians. They smiled and nodded.

"Ok, let's move out."

The back door of the shuttle opened while the entire team put on their helmets and finished checking each other's gear. The wind raced by and nearly pulled them out through the open door. Once everyone was ready and in position Lonan gave the thumbs-up sign and they all ran toward the door and jumped out into the night sky.

Elsewhere at the slave compound on the planet Trilon, one of the Seberians looked out across the main chamber of the compound. Down below he could see Helion soldiers helping people down from the slave racks and Leviathan soldiers lying on the floor shaking and convulsing.

"Base, come in. Mission's complete for team number four. We're on our way home," reported the Seberian soldier as he pulled a charge from his pack and set it on the control panel.

In another star system Helion team five had also just successfully completed their mission. Outside the Nemaron slave compound hundreds of slaves were being loaded into the Helion ship, the soldiers helping the last of them into the cargo bay. The engines fired as the crew prepared to takeoff.

"Team five loaded and we're on our way," reported the Helion pilot from the cockpit.

As the last few slaves loaded into the ship, one of the Helion soldiers was gunned down from several blasts within the building. That sent the rescued slaves running into the ship as Helion soldiers returned fire. An automated gun popped out of the top of the wing of the ship and took out seven Leviathan soldiers who had crept up from the other side of the building.

The last of the Helion soldiers jumped on board, and their spacecraft took off into the air. As they did, Leviathan soldiers ran from the building and fired up into the air and hit the hull of the shuttle. The Helion escort fighter hovered down into position and took out the Leviathan with Lonan's specialized electric rounds. The Helion shuttle and fighter both accelerated into the sky.

Moments later the compound exploded in an enormous blast as the Helion charges detonated.

The angels and demons were fully engaged in combat at the portal to heaven. Tekel fought in the front lines and was holding off three demons all at the same time. He was far stronger than any of them and more gifted in the use of the sword. The Leviathan soldiers continued to attack the angels who tried to ignore and throw them aside but when they got in their way the angels were forced to kill.

Suddenly, what appeared to be a shockwave entered the atmosphere and passed over the entire battlefield. As it reached the angels their eyes lit up simultaneously. They all took in a deep, refreshing breath. Even the stone angels seemed to be recharged by it.

As it passed over the demons and human Leviathan, they slowed. The red mist around their bodies dissipated and grew very faint. They all winced as if in pain and pulled back a few steps from the angels they were engaging.

Still sitting on his horse in the center of his side of the battlefield, Satan also felt the pain and cried out in frustration. "Those useless humans have lost more of my slaves. Abodile, come to me."

The demon left the ranks and flew to Satan's side.

"Take one of our soldiers with you and go to the Crule compound and make sure that it is not lost to the humans. We need that power."

"Yes, my lord," the demon replied, his head slightly bowed.

Satan looked across his army to see that their power had been diminished. The red mist was still present but had lost its intensity. They were not attacking with the same speed as before, and that troubled him.

"But before you go, I need you to finish something here. I'm afraid that these humans have outlived their usefulness. They're now taking and wasting precious power that our soldiers need. Destroy them and get our power back," ordered Satan as a grin grew on his face.

The demon turned and flew back toward the front lines of the battle field. He gave out a beastlike roar mixed with an ancient demon tongue. All the demons turned and looked at him and then turned and looked at the humans. Evil grins grew on their faces as they turned on the men that they had been fighting alongside. They attacked the Leviathan with no remorse or hesitation.

The humans tried to fight back, but they were no match for the demons' supernatural power and speed.

The angels stepped back and watched in disgust. One of them turned to Tekel and asked, "Sir, should we help the humans?"

"No. Leave them to their fate. We warned them," answered Tekel, sorrow gripping his heart.

The angels collected themselves, reformed their defensive lines, and watched in deep disappointment as the last of the humans were killed by Satan's army. The red mist covered the battle field as it poured from the dead bodies of the fallen Leviathan. This caused the demons to regain much of their strength. They breathed in the mist and the death and destruction; their eyes blazed as they turned their attention back to the angels.

"Attack!" screamed Satan, and his army of demons re-engaged their heavenly enemies.

In another star system Helion team six worked desperately to escape their failed rescue mission.

"Retreat!" yelled a Helion soldier as he ran from a squadron of Leviathan who were chasing him down. A shot in the back took him down.

The rest of his unit's escape was cut off by ten other Leviathan. The men stood helpless with nowhere to go as they were executed. This happened at the same moment that the slave racks all around them dropped. The slaves screamed. The red mist completely filled the air and the collection chamber pulsated with intense red light.

The angels and demons continued in their battle at the great gate. The speed of the sword fighting was incredibly fast as the demons were still filled with power from the death boost. The angels focused intensity just to keep up with their speed. Suddenly, the demons received another boost as the execution at another camp was successful. Their muscles flared and their eyes lit up with a bright-red light.

"Another failed mission," thought Tekel as he fought four demons at the same time.

This boost in power didn't phase the angels. They didn't shrink back in fear but rather focused more intently on each and every blade thrust.

Satan watched at a safe distance from the front lines. His eyes burned with rage as he saw the power and focus of his enemy. Despite the advantage that his army had from feeding on the pain and suffering of mankind, they were still far from reaching the portal. He began to fear that his battle would be lost. His mind drifted back to the war in heaven when he and his army lost and were expelled forever.

Filled with rage and fear, he jumped from his horse and flew toward Tekel in the front lines. Satan roared as he neared the battle line. Tekel heard him and jumped into flight to meet him in mid-air. They clashed directly above the river. They each pulled their swords and engaged in sword fighting that was faster and more intense than any other on the battle field. Shreds of fire and bolts of lightning flew across the battlefield as their blades collided.

Meanwhile Lonan and his team free fell through the air toward the compound far below them. They opened compact parachutes, which nearly stopped their descent immediately. Small jet packs fired very quietly as they leveled themselves out and came in for very soft landings on the flat roof of the compound.

Telgrin pulled a small device from his pack that allowed him to see through the roof electronically. Lonan took a look also as four of his soldiers went to work quietly disassembling a part of the roof and disarming the security system. By using Telgrin's device they were able to see the captives in the racks down below.

Once the team had opened the roof they all quietly climbed down into the ceiling below.

Inside the building they found themselves in the rafters of an enormous slave compound. High up against the ceiling they tried to gather on very narrow catwalks.

The hole that they had crawled in through was very near to the outer wall. The rest of the building stretched on for a long distance. On the far end they could see two collection chambers nearly touching the ceiling. They glowed with a solid red. As they peered down below they could see thousands of people hanging upside down in the racks. Below them were red, glowing pits of lava. Just below the racks, but above the lava, a system of crisscrossing metal walkways covered the enter building. They seemed to pass in-between the racks in a way that would not impede the slaves from being lowered down.

Lonan whispered into the mouthpiece of his head set as he addressed his team. "Ok, team two, you've got your orders. Lock those drop mechanisms as a failsafe. Team one with me to the command center. I want one Seberian to cover each team."

Team two was made up of six Helion soldiers and one Seberian. They spread out across the building, crawling like spiders through the webbing of the rafters. They went directly to the points where the massive rack systems attached to the ceiling. They immediately pulled tools from their packs and went to work.

Lonan and his team consisted of Telgrin, three other Helion soldiers, and one Seberian. They quietly made their way toward the center of the building where they could begin to see the control room down below them. It was a large room covered with glass on three sides. The remaining side had an elevator that went down several meters to the walkways and racks below. From the position of the control room the entire system of racks could be seen and monitored. Thousands of wires flowed up from the rack systems and all converged at the center of the building, where they went down into the ceiling of the command center.

"Wait, stop," whispered one of the Seberians.

The rest of the team froze.

Just down below him a massive demon glided through the spaces between the racks. His head turned back and forth as he patrolled the room. Only the Seberian was able to see him. The rest of the men looked on in silence as they desperately wondered what he had seen. While he slowly scanned the rest of the room he warned the team. "There are demons here."

"Great. How many?" asked Lonan.

"So far I've seen three."

"Ok, keep them off us. That's what you're here for," said Lonan. He turned and continued crawling toward the center of the building.

Down below Leviathan soldiers walked along the metal walkways on patrol. Lonan looked straight down below and saw nothing but lava and the very bottom of the rafter webbing to which he was clinging.

"Let's get to the command center quick," said Lonan as beads of sweat began to roll down his face.

Chapter 10

Back at the Helion base, Nemaron ground assault transports slowed their approach as they entered the planet's atmosphere. Many had made it past the Helion fighters. As they neared the surface they extended landing gear and fired smaller hover mode engines. The transports landed in a large, open plain nearly five kilometers away from the foot of the mountain. More and more Nemaron transports poured in; the Helion fighters did the best they could to shut them down, but they were overrun by the multitude of ships.

The first wave Nemaron fighters that had set up a defensive perimeter around the planet now started to move in and attack the Helion spacecraft. The Nemaron fleet numbered over two hundred, while the Helion fleet dwindled down to just over half their size. The Nemaron ships were more heavily armored, but the Helion fighters were lighter, faster, and more agile.

They had been successful in shutting down many Nemaron ground assault transports. Nearly thirty of them had been disabled and were now drifting off into space. But many had made it past and were now landing all across the valley in front of the Helion base. Large cargo bay doors opened on the backs of the Nemaron transports, and hundreds of Leviathan soldiers poured out. As the soldiers exited the ships they lined up in formations facing the Helion base.

Overhead the air battle continued as the Nemaron fighters engaged the Helienders' air defense. A few Helienders crashed into the side of the mountain in balls of flame as their fighters were shot down.

The rest of the Helion fleet still fought to keep as many of the Nemaron transports off the surface of the planet as possible while at the same time avoiding Nemaron fighters.

The Leviathan continued to pour out of the transports, but some of the heavier armored shuttles carried more than Leviathan. The larger Nemaron ships opened their bay doors to reveal tanks and artillery. The tanks rolled out and took positions just in front of the Leviathan infantry formations. The tanks stood nearly four meters tall and stretched six meters across. They had a quad track system that gave them increased turning ability and far greater overall agility. The turret mounted on top had dual cannons that fired 0.25 meter rounds. They also had smaller guns mounted on the sides that were designed for taking out infantry. The armor was extremely thick and could withstand very large caliber ammunition. Within moments nearly forty tanks had taken position and were taking aim at the Helion base.

The heavy Nemaron transports also carried long-range surface-to-surface field artillery. They were pulled out of the shuttles by six-wheeled solider transports and positioned far behind the tanks and Nemaron front line. Once in position they were stabilized by eight legs that folded down from the sides and pierced themselves into the ground. The canons were nearly seven meters long and immediately moved into correct position, ready to fire on the base.

Deep inside the mountain in the Helion command center, Kilgron and many of his commanders watched every movement of the invasion on the holographic imaging table. The rest of the soldiers in the command center were focused on giving directions to their fighters who were still trying desperately to stop the transports from landing.

"All squad leaders turn your attention to the heavy artillery that they're unloading," commanded Kilgron.

"Roger that," the Helion fleet commander answered. "You heard him. Units one and two, you focus on the groups to the north. Units three and four to the south. Units five and six stay focused on intercepting the incoming shuttles."

Units one and two flew away from the battlefield and to the north. They took on heavy fire from the Nemaron fighters as they moved away from the battle to regroup and set up formation. Each unit had eight fighters remaining. They collected themselves and formed a v-shaped configuration as they turned back toward the battlefield. The fleet commander piloted the fighter in the center of the formation.

"Unit one and two follow me," ordered the fleet commander. "Unit two, give us cover fire. Unit one, you're with me. Hit those artillery canons with all you've got. Switch over to destructive rounds. We're just destroying equipment here."

"Roger that," answered the rest of the Helion pilots. They finished turning back to the battlefield and rapidly approached the Nemaron front lines. As they got closer the Nemaron soldiers turned their large-caliber surface-to-air guns on the approaching Helion fighters.

Rounds flew past the Helienders as they approached the lines. Unit two targeted the surface-to-air guns while unit one opened fire on the canons. As the two units took their first pass, they hit and destroyed three of the artillery canons but also took on some damage from the Nemaron guns.

The enemy's line ran from north to south, so the Helion fighter units one and two focused their attack on the northern half while units three and four attacked the southern side of the line. Units three and four had executed a similar attack run. They, however, only took out two Nemaron canons and also lost one Helion fighter. It was shot down by surface-to-air guns and crashed into a heavy Nemaron transport that was just coming in for a landing. Both ships burst into flames and sent shrapnel flying across the battlefield.

Helion fighter units one through four continued their attacks on the Nemaron field artillery and took out several more, but Nemaron quickly pulled in more fighters to engage the Helienders in combat high above the battle field.

Deep inside the Helion command center, Kilgron turned to one of the soldiers. "Prepare all countermeasure cannons."

"Yes, sir."

Kilgron grabbed the intercom microphone. "Attention, all ground troop commanders!"

Hundreds of Helion soldiers ran around the main hangar as they worked to finish loading the AUVS while Kilgron's voice boomed over the loudspeaker.

"The enemy forces have landed. Deploy all ground forces."

The Helienders were loading the last of the electric rounds that Lonan and Telgrin had engineered. All the weapons had been ungraded to use this new type of non-lethal round. All the vehicles and equipment had also been changed over to hydro-cell power system, which meant that the enemy catalyst missiles would not have any effect on their power supply.

The infantry soldiers were dressed in their heavier body armor and helmets and began to line up in formations in the center of the hangars. The AUVS and Stingers were lined up nearer to the hanger doors and were ready to roll out. The last of the infantry soldiers loaded into the backs of the AUVS and the ramps pulled up into place and then locked and sealed.

Averine threw her last medic pack into her AUV as her fellow medics filed into the back of the transport. The AUVS had very heavy armor and the insides were lined with seats that backed up against the outer wall of the haul of the transport. Each of the medics also carried rifles as well as their medic packs.

As Averine strapped on her helmet she looked around the hangar to see her fellow Helienders finishing preparations. Her heart swelled with pride to see the precision of the soldiers and their equipment. She and these soldiers had been on countless rescue missions that had freed thousands of helpless people trapped in the Nemaron clutches. Many of the soldiers she saw standing in formation had been some of those who had been rescued. She looked inside the AUV at her fellow medics. Nearly half of them under her command in this unit had been rescued from Nemaron camps.

Her heart was filled with gratitude. She was honored to have been a part of their rescue and to now fight alongside these people to protect their home. And that thought brought her back to reality. The battle had come home and it was time to get to work. As she stepped into the back of the AUV she looked far across the hanger to see Cloin standing as the lone Seberian among an army of Helion soldiers.

Cloin had been ready for battle for some time. She stood beside a motorcycle transport that she would be driving out onto the field. Her blades had been sharpened and rested sheathed on her back. Her rifle had been upgraded to use both the electric rounds and demon heavenly armor rounds, which could easily penetrate the demon's thick body armor.

She sat on the motorcycle and watched as the Helienders prepared, impressed with their order and precision. Her mind drifted back to the many rescue missions that she and her fellow Seberians had helped them to accomplish. She knew that the Helienders where noble and caring people, and she thought back to what God had told her back in the clearing in the mountain. He had told her that the time had come for more people to draw near to him and also become Seberians. Cloin wondered about the Helienders and what God might have in store for them.

Out on the battlefield hundreds more Leviathan unloaded from the transports while the Nemaron soldiers finished unloading their field artillery cannons and where taking aim at the Helion base.

One of the Nemaron commanders sat in the safety of a heavily fortified mobile command center that had been placed at the back to the Nemaron forces. From within this bunker the Nemaron commanders could see and manage all aspects of the battlefield and their forces.

"Sir, all canons are on line and ready to fire," a soldier reported.

"Excellent," the commander answered. "Target the base of the mountain and fire."

Seconds later the massive cannons shook the ground as they fired their missiles at the Helion base. Immediately countermeasure missiles were launched from the mountain. Each of the Nemaron missiles were intercepted and neutralized by the Helion countermeasures. They fell to the ground as spheres and steamed as the explosion was neutralized. The blasts had been completely contained.

"Fire at will," barked the Nemaron cannon commander.

Thirty missiles were fired at the base while at the same moment the Helion hangar doors slowly opened. All the Helion ground units rolled out on the landing pads and then down onto the field below the mountain base. The AUVS and Stingers advanced toward the Nemaron army and the now-thousands of Leviathan soldiers standing in formations beside the enormous four track tanks that made up the enemy front lines.

The Helion infantry ran in formation behind the AUVS as the Stingers accelerated and moved out to the front of Helion forces.

The Leviathan soldiers stood in their heavy armor with the red, boomerang-shaped amulet built into their chest plates growing intensely. The red light grew and reflected up onto the full face guards of their helmets. They shifted back and forth in anticipation of the battle to come. The evil demonic power within them had created a lust and thirst for death. They were eager to engage and could feel the moment coming.

The Helion infantry, armed with electric round rifles, continued to pour out of the hangar doors. Cloin also rolled out on her motorcycle and sat for a moment on the edge of the landing platform as the Helienders ran past. She looked up into the sky to see the Helion fighters engaging the Nemaron aircraft. She hoped to see her father's ship coming in with reinforcements in the form of their fellow Seberians. She saw no sign of him. She looked down at the scanners on the console of the motorcycle and saw no indication of his shuttle.

"Okay, Father, any time now," she said. She pulled on her gloves and tightened the wristbands. The whites of her eyes glowed with a piercing white light as she gazed across the wide valley below to see the Nemaron army's front line. She smiled a little, twisted the throttle, and revved the engine. She popped the machine in gear, lifted her foot, and raced off toward the battlefield, weaving through the Helion infantry and past the AUVS toward the front of the Helion lines.

Inside the Nemaron command bunker several soldiers monitored the battle. "Sir, their ground forces have taken the field," reported one of the soldiers.

"Send in our infantry," ordered the commander.

Out on the Nemaron front lines the Leviathan infantry unit leaders received their orders and at the same moment yelled, "Attack!" All of the Leviathan soldiers who had been standing in formation now charged at the Helion forces that were riding out to meet them. The Leviathan ran across the battlefield at incredible speed while just meters over their heads more Helion countermeasures intercepted the fresh batch of Nemaron missiles. Most of the countermeasures did their job, but two of the enemy rockets made it through and hit the side of the mountain with an enormous force.

Everyone inside the command center braced themselves as the impact violently shook the entire Helion base. The lights flickered for a few minutes, then soldiers tried to assess the damage. Deeper in the mountain the women and children also felt the impact. The children screamed and cried as their mothers drew them near and tried to console them. The lights went out, and the mountain base shook violently.

Back out on the battlefield, another group of thirty Leviathan unloaded from a transport. They each had larger metal packs on their backs. As they unloaded they spread out across the northern end of the Nemaron front line. They each adjusted some controls built into arms of their body armor, which caused metal wings to unfold from their sides. Seconds later small jet engines lifted them off the ground. They all hovered for a few seconds and then in unison all took off toward the Helion base.

At the foot of the mountain the dust finally started to clear at the spot where the missiles had hit the base. The metal of the fortress wall was now fully exposed. It had been covered by a thick layer of dirt and vegetation but was now visible, charred and dented.

Chapter 11

B ack at Lonan's slave compound, Lonan and his team continued inching their ways along through the ceiling rafters until they stopped just above the command center. Without a sound they pulled ropes from their packs and attached them to the rafters. Once everyone was ready they all simultaneously repelled down onto the ceiling of the command center five meters below them.

The command center was a room built up above the racks, and its walls were made of glass on three sides. This allowed the soldiers inside to look out and monitor all activity in the racks. The fourth wall was made up of the elevator, which was the only way in or out of the center. Inside, the room was filled with control panels and eight Leviathan monitoring the systems.

Without any of the Leviathan noticing, one of the ceiling tiles pulled back and three small spheres hovered down to the floor. They spread out around the room silently and positioned themselves behind the unsuspecting Leviathan. Then they opened and sent out electrical current that knocked out all of the enemy soldiers. When each of them rolled over and hit the floor, Lonan and his men quickly repelled down through the ceiling.

The Seberian, however, didn't pass down through the ceiling. Off in the distance he saw a large demon on patrol. He was heading toward them, so the Seberian decided to head him off before he found Lonan and his team inside the control room.

Telgrin and another Heliender immediately went to work hacking the computer system. Telgrin's eyes got big as he looked at the Nemaron control station. "The drop sequence has been initiated. We only have ten minutes," Telgrin whispered into his com. "And a lot of codes to bypass."

"Get to work," said Lonan. He prepared charges and set them in strategic places around the room.

Just then, without anyone noticing, one of the Leviathan stood up in the middle of the room. He grabbed one the Helion soldiers and threw him against the opposite wall. Lonan drew his rifle and fired electric rounds and took down the Leviathan. As his body hit the floor, another of the enemy soldiers silently rose up behind Lonan and grabbed him. He lifted Lonan from the floor and without any effort threw him across the room. Lonan slammed against the elevator door and dented it. As he stumbled to his feet and tried to clear his head he yelled to his men. "Get him!"

The other Helienders jumped to their feet while Telgrin worked frantically to hack the system and shut down the execution. The Helienders drew their weapons and fired the electric rounds. With his incredible speed the Leviathan was able to dodge many of the bullets and grab the nearest Heliender, whose neck he broke just seconds before some of the electric rounds caught him and sent him to the floor convulsing.

Lonan stumbled to his feet and prepared to enter the fight when the elevator door opened behind him to reveal Devakin and six more Leviathan.

"Sound the alarm," barked Devakin. "And search the building. Let's see how many of these little maggots have crawled in."

One of the Leviathan reached over and hit an alarm button on the wall of the command center. Immediately the alarm sounded throughout the compound.

Down in the main chamber twelve Leviathan came running in from patrolling the outside. The alarm started to awaken the slaves hanging in the racks. They looked around, trying to see straight. Some gathered the strength to call out for help.

The Seberians jumped down from the ceiling and landed on the catwalks that passed in between the rack system. They landed just in front of the Leviathan as they ran toward the command center in the middle of the building.

Up in the rafters the rest of the Helion team scrambled frantically, wrapping thick cables around the lever system that would release the racks and drop the slaves into the lava below.

"Hurry up, they know we're here!" As the Helion soldier spoke he looked around to see that the rack system was divided into three parts. They were just finishing locking down the first one. "We've got to hurry," he said to the other Helion soldier working with him. "Do you see what I see?"

The other soldier looked up to see that there were two other mechanical levers that would lower the racks. The problem was that they were on the other sides of the building, nearly fifty meters away. They would need to quickly crawl through the rafter system without being detected and without falling to their deaths into the lava below.

"Great," the second Heliender said. "Here." He handed the other a second pack of equipment. "You take that one and I'll this one over here."

"You got it. Let's go," said the first Heliender. They both crawled and swung their ways toward the other drop levers.

In the command center Telgrin pulled a remote monitor under a desk for cover while he continued to work to hack the system and shut down the execution. The rest of the Helienders did the best they could to fight off the Leviathan. Some of their rounds were dodged by the enemies' superhuman speed, but some of them hit their mark and sent them to the floor.

Devakin slowly walked toward Lonan, who pulled his rifle and fired. Devakin dodged the first two but was hit by the third. The current passed throughout his body. Devakin fell to his knees then slowly started to laugh. He had so much of Satan's evil fear feeding power in him that he was able to withstand the electrical current. He stood up and charged Lonan. Devakin threw a punch that hit him so hard that he flew across the room.

"Why did you come here?" asked Devakin walking slowly toward Lonan, who lay nearly unconscious on the floor. "You should have just stayed home and minded your own business."

Lonan rolled over in pain as he struggled to catch his breath while at the same time searching on the floor for his rifle. When he finally found it he pulled himself to his feet and took aim at Devakin, who was picking up speed as he walked in Lonan's direction. The powerful Leviathan commander grinned and raised his hands, inviting Lonan to take a shot.

Lonan pulled the trigger and released a wave of ten rounds into Devakin's chest. The rounds hit and sent a tremendous amount of current through his body. This stopped him for a second. As the current dissipated, he began to laugh again. He reached up and opened his jacket to reveal an angelic chest plate over his Leviathan one.

"Do you like it? I got it from one of your friends the angels. Of course he was dead when I took it."

Lonan looked on in amazement as he scrambled to reach into his leg pocket for the heavenly metal-penetrating rounds that where distinguishable from the others by their red casing. He loaded the clip, but before he could lock it into place Devakin ran to him, ripped the rifle from his hands, and threw it across the room. It hit the floor of the elevator. As it did the clip popped out and skidded across the floor. Just then the elevator door closed.

Devakin then picked Lonan up into the air by his throat and punched him in the face so hard that he was knocked unconscious.

Meanwhile, in the center of the battlefield on the planet Helion, the Leviathan and Helienders continued on their collision course. The Leviathan ran at half their normal speed as if they were waiting and savoring the enjoyment to come.

The Helion soldiers continued down the gradual slope toward their enemy. The stingers led the charge with the AUVS close behind and with the Helion infantry running behind them. When they reached optimal range for their weapons, the Stinger gunners opened fire with their four-centimeter electric rounds. They had these in the top-mounted, quad-barrel guns that sat just above the drivers' cockpits.

Ten Stingers were spread out across the front of the Helion defensive lines and rocketed toward the invading army. The electric rounds poured across the open battlefield and cut through the Leviathan ranks. As the rounds hit they immediately took out the first three lines of Leviathan. The soldiers fell to the ground unconscious with the electrical current pouring over their bodies. The next round of Leviathan didn't hesitate but continued in their attacking run toward the Helion lines.

At that same moment back in the Nemaron command bunker a soldier analyzed the results of their attack.

"Sir, we've exposed the outer walls of their base," he reported, pointing to his control monitor.

His commanding officer looked over his shoulder at the monitor. "Good. Focus all our fire power on that location."

"Yes, sir."

At the back of the Nemaron lines the field artillery that remained turned remotely as they rotated on their bases. They each targeted the area of the Helion base that had been exposed by their previous attack. In order from south to north, the cannons consecutively fired on the Helion base. Every six seconds another round was fired from the next massive cannon.

Inside the Helion base they could hear the consistent bombardment of the Nemaron field artillery. In the command center Kilgron leaned over one of the soldiers at a control panel. "Evacuate everyone in that wing of the base. If they break through we'll need to shut it all down."

"Roger that, sir," yelled a Helion soldier as he struggled to be heard over the constant bombardment of artillery attack.

Elsewhere in the Helion base men and women helped each other as they ran down the hallway. The lights flickered and debris hung from the ceiling as the base shook again from the impact of yet another well-placed missile.

In the Nemaron bunker the commanding officer turned to another monitor and called to Maginon's command shuttle.

"Sir. We should be finished with this slight resistance very soon. We have nearly penetrated their fortress walls. I believe you can send the mining shuttles, we'll have your work force momentarily."

Maginon sat in the pilot's chair on the bridge of the command shuttle as he received the message. He couldn't help but grin as he watched the attack on large monitors form the safety of his ship. "Very good. Launch the mining shuttles."

"Yes, sir," answered one of his soldiers there with him on the command deck.

Moments later the long, drill-shaped shuttles took off from hangars on the far back quarter of each of the ten Nemaron spacecraft. The Helion fighters were still engaging the Nemaron fighters as they fought to control the narrow strip of space that lay between the Nemaron carriers and the planet Helion. As the drill ships turned toward the planet they each were joined by three Nemaron fighters that escorted them through the outer-atmospheric battle.

Meanwhile, down in the center of the battlefield, the Helion forces had run out of space and the Leviathan infantry crashed on to the Helion Stingers like ocean waves overtaking rocky shores. The Leviathan poured over them and consumed most of the Stingers. They jumped on top and began to destroy them as they continued to plow through Leviathan ranks. The large wheels and suspension of the Stingers along with their wide metal battering ram mounted on the front rolled over and through many of the Leviathan. Most were knocked unconscious; however, several that were run over immediately jumped back to their feet and continued on their attack toward the Helion forces.

The Stingers that were not completely overtaken and destroyed by the thousands of Leviathan continued to lay down fire and electrify hundreds of the enemy soldiers. Those stingers that made it through the Leviathan charge stopped short of attacking the line of Nemaron tanks. They knew that their weapons would be useless against the tanks' armor, so they turned back and re-engaged the Leviathan from behind.

As the AUVS neared the Leviathan forces they fired their side-mounted guns. These rounds had been engineered to capture as many invaders as possible. As the round flew through the air and neared the enemy, the outer casing peeled off and in the process pulled open a ten-meter-wide net. Each net was made of a heavy yet flexible metal mesh that spun and expanded as it flew through the air. Once they landed they covered twenty to thirty advancing Leviathan. At the moment the nets made contact the electrical current was discharged and the Leviathan all received the non-lethal jolt of electricity. All the Leviathan within the nets immediately fell to the ground.

The Helion soldiers driving the AUVS cheered as they saw the success of the net system. Everyone inside the command center also cheered as they watched from within the safety of the base.

Just at that moment Cloin rode in from the northern end of the battlefield. A clearing had been created from two electric nets taking out nearly seventy Leviathan. As she approached she hit a large mound of dirt and launched herself and her bike into the air. While she flew forty meters she pulled her rifle and fired electric rounds on the army of Leviathan that still numbered in the thousands. Her mind was attuned to every movement on the battlefield. She could see and hear everything that was happening and was able to process it so quickly that she could nearly see everything happening in slow motion. As she fired each round she watched each and every one hit its direct target. The Leviathan armor was weaker at the base of the neck, so each of her shots were directed for this one spot.

When the rounds hit the Leviathan received a more direct, and more potent, jolt of electrical current due to the lighter armor around the neck. Each of the Leviathan she hit was unconscious before their bodies touched the ground. In that way she took out another thirty enemy soldiers before she landed in the center of the clearing. Her bike landed with such a great force that she completely compressed the suspension. She rolled on into the clearing and was surrounded on three sides by enemy soldiers.

She calmly pulled her leg back over the motorcycle and extended the center stabilizer, which left the bike vertical and ready for her to jump back on at any time. She turned toward the hundreds of Leviathan soldiers who were now charging in her direction. The rest of the battle continued on the southern end as the Stingers and AUVS tried to take out as many enemy soldiers as possible. But all the Leviathan on this northern end of the charging infantry turned their attention to this lone women solider.

As the Leviathan advanced they all suddenly crouched down and released a horrific and deadly roar. They could now sense whom they were fighting. The holy power of God so filled Cloin that the demonic power within the Leviathan recoiled from her. They could feel her power, and it hurt them physically. The pain made them want to run, but the evil in them pushed them to want to destroy her. With an inner turmoil of both hate and fear the Leviathan charged full speed at Cloin.

As the enemy drew in closer she could sense all that was happening on the battlefield. The Nemaron artillery continued to bombard the exposed corner of the base on the far end of the field. The Helion and Nemaron fighters were still locked in endless mid-air battle. She could see and sense everything that was going on around her with extremely heightened sensitivity. As the Leviathan charged in her direction she could see each and every movement of each soldier as they came forward. With one fluid motion she pulled her rifle and fired in a continuous stream across the front lines of the Leviathan. One by one she took down each of them as she fired from right to left and then back to the right. Those who tried to dodge her rounds found themselves only jumping into her line of fire. The power of God that surged through every cell of her body gave her the ability to anticipate the enemy's movements and fire in advance of where they would be.

She took down the first three rows of Leviathan until she had emptied that clip. In one lightning fast motion she dropped the empty and inserted the new clip and only missed two seconds of firing. She laid down three more rows of Leviathan and finally ran out of ammunition. When that happened she threw the rifle to the side and pulled her two meter-long blades from the sheaths on her back. She knelt down on one knee and held the blades low to the ground. She bowed her head for a moment and when see raised it up again her eyes burned with a white-hot light.

A few of the Helion soldiers fighting on that side of the battlefield could see Cloin as she knelt there with an army of lighting-fast Leviathan running in her direction. To the Heliender's eyes the battle seemed to be a blur. All the movements of both Cloin and the Leviathan were so fast that their unaided human eyes could only see bits and pieces. They stood amazed and tried not to lose focus on their own battles at hand. But the fact remained that they couldn't believe the speed of the movement that they saw.

From Cloin's perspective, or of that of the Leviathan, the battle appeared at a slower than normal speed. As she raised her head she also leapt into the air nearly three meters. When she landed she was only half a meter from the front line of Leviathan that was charging her. As she touched the ground she spun in a tornado a blade strikes. All the Leviathan that were within three meters of her lost their red, glowing amulet that gave them their demonic power. She cut and tore them from their armor so fast that they could barely react. As the fear-feeding amulet hit the ground, so too dropped the Leviathan to their knees. The evil demonic power began to drain from their bodies, and the pain of that process was immense. The men cried out in agony as the black blood running through the veins in the whites of their eyes returned back to a normal red color.

Before another group of Leviathan could jump over those lying on the ground, Cloin jumped backward fifteen meters to a safe spot on a hill. When she touched down she landed in a kneeling position. With her head still facing the ground she said, "I was beginning to wonder when you were going to get here."

Just then her father Armon stepped up over the hill and stood beside her. He was dressed in his complete black body armor. He held one of the Helion rifles and also carried a blade on his hip. "I'm sorry it took so long. It seems that some of our Seberian brothers need a lot of time to pack."

At that moment Eliune of Galaxy 55x8 and his thirty Seberians stepped up over the hill. Eliune looked out across the battlefield to see the thousands of Leviathan attacking the Helion forces. He couldn't hide his smile. "If I'd known you had this type of partying waiting, we would have been here a lot sooner."

Chapter 12

Outside the base a squad of Helion fighters flew in a tight formation as they turned back for another attack run on the Nemaron ground forces. "Follow me in. Take out as many of their cannons as you can," ordered the squad leader.

The fighters came in low and locked their targeting systems on the massive surface mounted cannons that were bombarding the mountain side and Helion ground forces. As they weaved thought the rounds flying through the air they were able to take out another five Nemaron cannons.

As the Helion squad passed over the center of the Nemaron side of the battlefield, they picked up some unwanted attention. A group of five Nemaron soldiers equipped with the winged jet packs took to the air. Immediately they opened fire on the Helion fighters in an attempt to clear the battlefield. The Nemaron jet packs were able to match the Helion full-size fighter's speed, but due to their size and design they were far more agile.

The Heliender pilots tried desperately to lose their pursuers as they took on more and more direct hits to the back of their ships. Due to the smaller size the Nemaron jetpacks couldn't carry heavy armor or weapons, but what they had was beginning to cause too much damage. One of their shots caught a Helion fighter in a weakened spot in its armor. Immediately he caught fire and crashed into the side of the mountain.

Down on the battlefield Cloin, Armon, Eliune, and his thirty Seberian soldiers stood on a hill overlooking the battlefield.

Armon turned to the others. "The rest of the Helion forces are working to shut down the slave camps. When they do, these Leviathan will lose some power. But until that happens it looks like we have a lot of work to do."

The Seberians watched the battle; the bulk of the Leviathan forces had reached the line of AUVS. The Helienders continued to fire their electric nets and six-centimeter rounds from the top turret mounted on the AUVS. The sheer number of Leviathan, however, overpowered all the weapons of the Helion forces. Within moments the Leviathan had swarmed the Helion vehicles. Each AUV was covered with nearly twenty Leviathan who were shooting, punching, and tearing through the vehicle armor.

Behind the lines of AUVS the Helion infantry came running onto the battlefield. They each pulled up their non-firing hand and engaged the shield feature that was built into the forearm of their body armor. The shields were an energy-based devise that emitted from a powerful generator carried on their backs. Once energized and fully extended, the shields stood one meter tall and half a meter wide. They were strong enough to deflect most rounds that were fired from a rifle or pistol.

As the Helion infantry engaged they fired their electric rounds. They were able to hit some of the enemy soldiers, but the Leviathan were able to move so incredibly fast that they dodged many of the rounds and crashed into the infantry lines. Their speed and superhuman strength was far too much for the Helion soldiers to handle. Many of the Helienders were killed as the army of Leviathan continued to pour over the AUVs and through the Helion lines of defense.

Cloin stood and turned to the others. "Now they definitely need our help."

With that all of the small band of thirty-three Seberians ran with superhuman speed and charged the front lines of the Leviathan. Like shadows shifting across the ground they moved in and defended the Helion soldiers. Their attacks on the Leviathan where swift and appeared to be effortless. With faster-than-sight motion they engaged in very close quarters hand-to-hand combat with the demonically powered army. The Seberians used their blades and fists to subdue the enemy to the point that they could destroy and remove the red amulet embedded in their chest plates and skin. The Seberians moved through the Leviathan lines, leaving a trail of soldiers laying on the ground writhing in pain as the demonic power poured out of their bodies.

The Helienders took advantage of the fact that some of the Leviathan had pulled their attention to the Seberians. This allowed them the unique moment to land some electric rounds on the enemy.

Just then an explosion rocked the battlefield just behind the line of AUVs. Both Helion and Leviathan bodies went flying through the air as a crater opened in the ground. The Nemaron tanks had opened fire. The Helion infantry scrambled to take cover behind the AUVs or any small hills that lay between them and the Nemaron line of tanks. Within just a few moments an AUV that was returning fire on the tanks exploded in an enormous ball of fire and metal.

As Armon finished disarming three Leviathan he turned back to the other Seberians and yelled, "Eliune!"

"We're on our way," Eliune yelled back as he threw a Leviathan amulet to the ground and signaled to five of his soldiers. The six of them turned from the Leviathan they were fighting and ran directly for the Nemaron front lines. All of the tanks had now started to fire, and explosions they created on the battlefield left three-meter-deep craters. The Seberians dodged many rounds that passed them as they neared the Nemaron tanks.

Once they reached them, the Seberians immediately went to work destroying the tanks. They started on the north end and converged on one tank at a time as one unit. One Seberian would pry open the top hatch with super human strength and drop in a smoke grenade while the others would break and disassemble each and every gun. From time to time some Leviathan infantry that had been stationed in the back lines behind the tanks would attack. But each time they were quickly disarmed and left writhing in pain. As the Nemaron soldiers inside the tanks crawled out choking, they were quickly apprehended and taken out of the battle.

Back on the battlefield Averine and the soldiers in her AUV continued to lay down cover fire for the Helion infantry from the back lines on the southern end of the battlefield. They, along with a few other AUVs that had not yet been overrun by the Leviathan, were able to take out a few of the tanks before the Seberians reached them.

On the far side to the mountain, Sevran and his team flew in for a landing after returning from their rescue mission. From a distance within the cockpit he could see the vast battlefield below.

The Nemaron cannons continued to fire on the Helion forces and mountain side. Most of the Nemaron missiles were captured by the Helion counter measures, but several were not, and the damage and death totals were escalating.

Sevran still had two fighter escorts who now turned immediately and entered the mid-air dog fight happening not too far above the battlefield. While they joined the fight Sevran landed his shuttle in one of the main hangers. "We need to get out there." He radioed in, "Base, get my bike ready."

As they entered the hangar a team of fifteen Helion medics rushed to Sevran's shuttle as it slowly touched down. As soon as the door opened they rushed in with floating stretchers to unload the rescued slaves.

Sevran jumped from the main cockpit and ran to a soldier who was rolling his bike to him.

"Your bike, sir."

"Thanks," said Sevran. He pulled on his helmet and grabbed more rounds for his rifle which he then slung over his shoulder.

Back out on the battlefield the Leviathan had unfortunately become aware of the nets, and some were able to dodge them as well as the electric rounds. As they continued to advance they also pulled their rifles and opened fire on the Helion infantry. They killed large numbers of soldiers, and many bodies lay dead across the battlefield. The AUV armor was strong enough to repel the fire of the Leviathan infantry. But the enemy force that had taken to the air with jetpacks had now turned their attention off the Helion fighters and onto the ground forces.

Just then, Sevran and a unit of six other Helion soldiers rode out of the main hangar on their motorcycles. They were heavily armored and full of ammunition as they road up onto a hill that overlooked the battlefield. From there they could see the two advancing forces and the widespread damage that the Leviathan were causing. Sevran could see that there were already many wounded and dead and that the casualties would continue to escalate. They could also see that the Leviathan with jetpacks were now causing much of the damage.

"We need to take out those guys with the packs. Let's go," ordered Sevran, and he and his men took off down the hill toward the battle.

As they approached the battlefield they picked up a great deal of speed while also beginning to take on enemy fire. Sevran steered toward a large mound on the backside of the battlefield and hammered down on the throttle. He hit the mound and launched himself thirty meters through the air. As he left the lip of the mound, he threw the bike sideways. With his forward canons he targeted the jet pack of one of the Leviathan. His round hit its mark, and the Leviathan's jetpack exploded while he crashed to the ground.

While still in midair, Sevran reached back with his left hand and grabbed his pistol, which he used to take out another jetpack Leviathan approaching from the opposite side. Then Sevran swung the bike straight again just in time to land on the downhill-sloped side of a mound.

The men in his unit also took to the air and began to take out many Leviathan as their motorcycle targeting systems destroyed the jetpacks. This drew a lot of attention from the enemy forces, and soon they were converging on Sevran and his team. Before long the Leviathan had swarmed to them and they were surrounded. Within moments Sevran began to lose men as the Leviathan closed in.

Sevran pulled out to the side of the area to get a clear run. He found a good clearing and without slowing down re-approached the area where the Leviathan were converging. He hit a large mound and launched his bike over the battlefield. As he did he pulled the bike into a barrel roll and backflip combination. He switched on the targeting system to fire everything. Tracer rounds flew in all directions as his bike flipped through the air. Many of his shots landed and took down several Leviathan.

From the backside of the battlefield the Nemaron canons launched ten missiles simultaneously. All of them where aimed directly at the exposed section of the Helion base wall. Counter measures launched from the mountain base and intercepted all but three of the Nemaron missiles. Those three hit with a tremendous impact and blew a hole in the metal wall of the Helion fortification. As the dirt and smoke began to clear they could see directly into the base.

Inside the Helion command center everyone shook from the impact as the lights flickered. Over the loud speaker they could hear, "Base has been breached. Repeat, outer wall of base has been breached."

Chapter 13

Out on the battlefield the Leviathan continued to attack the Helion infantry in hand-to-hand combat. They were no match for the evil supernatural speed and power of the Leviathan, who killed many of the Helion men with ease. The Helion soldiers mounted on motorcycles, however, had a slight advantage in that they were able to outrun the Leviathan. They and the AUVs were still able to take out some of the enemy soldiers.

Another Nemaron ship entered the atmosphere and came in for a landing. It was a mining shuttle. It landed on the far outside of the battlefield in an upright position with its drill facing down. Enormous mechanical arms came out from the side and stabilized the spacecraft. Then the drill located in the center began to rotate as it inched closer to the ground.

The soldiers of Helion fought desperately to stop the Leviathan advance, but their enemy was too strong for them. Many were forced to retreat back into the cover of the AUVs. The soldiers on motorcycles lay down cover fire as the infantry soldiers tried to regroup. The AUV gunners continued to take out Leviathan with electric rounds and nets.

Many of the Leviathan were still on the tops of the AUVs, trying to break their way in. They shot numerous rounds at the seams in the hull of the AUVs and began to pry open doors with blades on the ends of their rifles and their bare hands.

On the other side of the battlefield a large force of Leviathan broke off from the rest and ran toward the hole that had been blasted in the side of the mountain base. From inside her

AUV Averine noticed them advancing and called to her driver. "We need to cover that hole. Take off now."

"Roger that," answered the driver. He turned the AUV and accelerated across the battlefield while running over a few Leviathan in the process. Two other AUVs followed to cut off the enemy force advancing toward the weak spot in the base wall.

The rest of the Helion AUVs continued to fire the electric nets at the Leviathan, which was quickly becoming less effective. The enemy had begun to spread out and was more aware of the nets, so fewer were being caught.

In the Helion base soldiers ran to inspect the damage where the base wall had been compromised. Debris fell from the ceiling and dust filled the air as they ran through the corridors; they rounded a corner to find the enormous hole. They could see tracer rounds enter through the opening and hit the wall on the far side. They could hear the battle raging on the outside and the clinking of the Leviathan body armor as they ran toward the hole.

"Get back to the main doors," shouted a Helion soldier. "Unit five take the west side, we'll take the east."

The two units ran down the hall way in opposite directions until they came to lockdown points. Once on the inside they closed the enormous metal doors and locked them. Then they took positions to defend against anything that might break through.

Back out on the battlefield a Nemaron sergeant called to his Leviathan through the com links, "Ok, enough killing. Collect these weaklings and bring them to the mine shuttle."

The Leviathan immediately began to tackle the Helion soldiers and tie their arms behind their backs. They pulled the soldiers from the motorcycles and broke through some of the AUVs and pulled the Helion soldiers from the vehicles. They tied them together in large groups and started to march them toward the mine shuttle.

Many of the Nemaron field artillery had not been taken out and were still firing from their position on the far side of the battlefield. One of the cannons turned and took aim at the three AUVs that were driving toward the hole in the base wall. The canon fired its missile and hit the ground just in front of Averine's AUV. The explosion created a huge crater and caused the AUV to flip over and crash.

From above the battlefield the Helion pilots converged on the area above the hole in the side of the base. They hovered down and fired thousands of electric rounds at the Leviathan who were quickly closing in on the hole. Their rounds took out many enemy soldiers, but the wave of Leviathan continued as thousands converged and prepared to enter the base.

Just then several Helion canons popped up out of the ground and fired the electrified nets at the wall of Leviathan. Two or three hundred hit the ground, but that didn't slow the enemy's progression. Within seconds they had reached the opening and poured into the Helion base.

Back at the AUV crash site the Helion driver labored to pull Averine from the wreckage as blood ran down his forehead and into his eye. She was wounded but still conscious. Her right leg was badly cut as was her right arm. The driver worked among the ruble that was his AUV at the bottom of the crater that the Nemaron missile formed. As he pulled away chunks of the hull that lay across Averine's body, a Leviathan ran by and stopped at the top of the crater. He peered down and found the two struggling under the rubble. He turned and started down the steep side of the hole in the ground.

The Helion driver pulled his pistol and fired at the approaching Leviathan, who quickly dodged the bullets. He ran to them at a lightning speed, kicked the pistol from the driver's hand, grabbed his head, and in an instant snapped his neck.

As the driver's dead body slumped to the ground, the Leviathan slowly turned to Averine.

"A woman," he said as he pulled up his com link. "Air unit. Come to these coordinates. I have the first addition to Maginon's collection."

Seconds later a Nemaron soldier mounted on a jet pack landed beside them in the crater. Averine struggled to collect her thoughts as her head recovered from the crash.

The Leviathan reached down to grab her.

She quickly drew her pistol and took aim only to have it pulled from her hands and crushed. The Leviathan picked up the debris and pulled her from the wreckage as if it was nothing.

"No! Put me down!" yelled Averine; she continued to try to clear her head while she punched and kicked as hard has she could.

The Nemaron soldier stepped forward and injected her with some form of sedative in the back of her neck. She instantly went limp. He then picked her up and flew off into the air and back toward the Nemaron command center.

Inside the Helion base, the Leviathan had filled the hallway and were beating on the metal doors that the Helienders had closed and barricaded. They also used large wrecking bars to pry the doors apart while the Helienders nervously waited on the other side with their weapons drawn and aimed at the back side of the door.

Just then the Helienders heard something above them in the ceiling. Suddenly one of the Leviathan fell through the ceiling and onto the floor in the middle of thirty Helion soldiers. They all opened fire with electric rounds. The Leviathan didn't have a chance against that many waiting soldiers and was quickly knocked out.

"Great. One down, a couple thousand to go," said the Helion squad leader, listening to more noises coming through the ceiling. "Lonan had better get those slave camps out of commission soon."

Back on the battlefield everything seemed to go into slow motion in Sevran's mind as he looked around and watched the devastation of his people. He was filled with despair as he saw Helienders lying dead on the ground and others being taken captive. The Seberians where continuing to fight and had taken out many Leviathan, but the numbers were just too great. They couldn't defeat the entire army of thousands of Leviathan with a small force of thirty-three.

He gathered his courage and took off toward a group of enemy soldiers. He managed to get off a few quick shots from his motorcycle when out of nowhere he was hit in the face with the butt of a Nemaron rifle.

The impact threw him from the bike and onto the ground while his motorcycle crashed into the back of an AUV. Sevran stumbled to his feet only to be injected in the neck with a sedative and to find himself back on the ground. As he lay there, slipping from consciousness, he could see Averine being carried through the air by a Nemaron soldier as he came in for a landing at their forward operating base. Then everything went black.

Meanwhile back on Lonan's rescue mission, Telgrin was still hiding underneath a desk in the Nemaron command booth high above the suspended slaves and lava below. He scrambled to hack the Nemaron system and shut down the execution sequence. He worked frantically as he whispered to himself, "We're not going to make it."

On the other side of the room Devakin grabbed Lonan by the throat and lifted him into the air. Lonan struggled to catch his breath as Devakin's grip tightened around his windpipe. Blood drained from Lonan's face as he looked over at the countdown clock to find it at 0:04.

"Looks like you are out of time," said Devakin with a grin.

Just then the clock turned to zero. Outside in the main chamber the slave rack dropping system went into motion. The retainers released and the racks began to free fall. They fell a half of meter and then stopped with a violent jerk. All the slaves cried out in fear.

Up in the ceiling the Helion unit leader watched as the cables that he and his men installed on the drop devices did their jobs to stop the descent.

"Yes, it worked," he shouted into his com link as he began to pack up his tools.

Suddenly a shadow arose from behind him. He was unaware and continued to pack his equipment. The shadow drew closer as demon wings extended from the side. In an instant the demon jumped from the shadow, grabbed him, and threw him to the walkways below.

In the command center Lonan was still being held in the air by his throat. Devakin looked out the window to see that the racks had stopped while at the same time the computer systems said, "System malfunction. System malfunction."

"What have you little maggots done?" grunted Devakin as he pulled a key from under his chest plate. He placed the key in the computer console and turned it. Seconds later the hydraulic drop system located high in the ceiling activated and began slowly lowering all the racks.

Lonan kicked Devakin in the face several times, but it did nothing. He only laughed as a single drop of black blood ran down his lip.

Then Devakin threw Lonan across the room. His back hit a large glass window and shattered it instantly. As Lonan fell backward helplessly, his mind went into slow motion. He could see thousands of shards of glass as he slowly flipped backward headfirst toward the open lava pit below, with nothing to stop him.

As he fell he passed by one of the slave racks. The slaves were hanging upside down; he was looking at them face to face. The nearest slave was a young woman. She tried to reach out to help him. He reached for her hand, but they were just centimeters from each other; he could not reach her.

Then in a split second his mind went back to the slave compound where his wife and brother had been held captive some weeks earlier. In his mind's eye he could see himself silently creeping along the outside of the slave execution chamber. As he passed one of the racks, a little girl looked over at him. Her eyes were glazed over with a milky-white haze. She reached out her hand for help as he passed. When their eyes locked, Lonan felt every muscle in his body freeze. He stopped and stared in horror at the sight of her in bondage.

Suddenly he was ripped back to reality as he continued to fall headfirst toward the lava. The little girl's face changed to the woman that now hung in the racks reaching out to him. He strained every muscle and reached as far as he could, but the distance was too great to reach the woman's hand. He continued to fall with nothing but lava beneath him.

Back at the great gate Satan and his demons had begun to push the angels back as they crept toward the portal to heaven. Tekel and Satan continued in sword battle. Satan seemed to have a speed advantage as the red pulsated in his eyes. Tekel, however, remained calm and focused.

Then suddenly one of the stone angels roared out in frustration as he was swarmed by fifty demons half his size. Tekel looked over to find him swinging his massive stone arms and his blade wreathed in lighting. He was trying desperately to hit one of his attackers. The demons were so fast and powerful, though half his size, they were able to land some painful blows. Then the stone angel was able to catch two underfoot, only to have them replaced by two more.

"You see brother?" sneered Satan. "It's only a matter of time until we enter through that gate. You've failed your precious God and his foul little humans."

While he and Satan each caught their breath, Tekel looked off into the night sky with heavy heart and mind as he peered at one particularly bright star.

Back at the slave compound Lonan continued to fall through the air while reaching out for the hand of the young woman in the slave racks when suddenly he slipped into a vision. Time seemed to stop, and instantly he was transported to the planet where his parents were killed. He looked around in confusion as he stood in the field of angel and demon armor. The sky was a strange orange and red and the clouds flew across the landscape at an unusually fast pace. He stood in complete silence, which he felt was strange considering how fast the clouds were moving.

Suddenly Lonan heard a clear voice: "You need to know that it was not my fault that your parents died. I never intended for this evil and death."

Lonan spun around, searching for the person talking. He found no one around but for some reason was not surprised. "Why? Everywhere I look, all I see is suffering, death, and destruction. Why do you let this happen?"

"Aren't you exaggerating? I believe you see more than death and destruction. You see life, love, and hope."

Images of Averine, Sevran, and Telgrin flashed in Lonan's mind.

"Don't you see humanity's responsibility and involvement in the state of your worlds? All of you have the power to resist the enemy. I gave you the freedom to choose. I want to help you, but you need to trust me. Together we can help this world."

Lonan hung his head and then fell to his knees. "This is too much. I have to take care of my family. I have to protect Averine and Sevran. But I can't. I can't even take care of myself." Lonan buried his head in his hands. "I can't do this myself. I need your help."

Instantaneously the wind swirled around his body as he knelt there in the middle to the ancient battlefield. He looked up to see the planet he was on gradually disappearing. Then, in an instant, he was back in the slave compound falling through the air, staring in the eye of the young girl in the slave rack. Suddenly his eyes filled with an intense white light and he received a jolt of power throughout his body. At this point he was falling past the metal-suspended walkway behind him. He reached backward with all of his strength to try to grab hold of one of the supports. His reach was short by just a few centimeters.

On the other side of the slave chamber Balim was still fighting an enormous demon that had him held in a head lock. As Balim struggled to breathe, his eyes suddenly blazed with white light. He received a boost of power that allowed him to flip the demon off his back. Balim then thrust his hand in Lonan's direction, which sent a shockwave across the chamber. When it reached Lonan, it gave him the small nudge he needed to finally reach the metal support bar.

Lonan dangled by one hand as he collected himself and looked around. Just ten meters below lay the pool of lava. He pulled himself up and wrapped his legs around other supports.

His eyes still blazed with white light as he looked over to see Balim catching his breath. The angel made eye contact and nodded to Lonan in approval.

With his sword raised high, the demon attacked Balim from behind. Without looking Balim pulled his blade and blocked the demon's sword. The demon was confused by such a well-placed defense while looking in the other direction.

Lonan was also confused because he could see the demon. Not perfectly, but he could at least see his shadowed outline in a haze. Lonan pulled himself up and crawled to the top of the walkway. As the slave racks continued to slowly lower toward the lava he looked around the slave chamber to find that his vision had changed. He was able to see one of the Seberians fighting an enormous demon in sword battle. They moved at a speed that was beyond human, but Lonan was able to see it all. He looked farther up in ceiling and found another demon flying through the air and heading toward some of his men.

Lonan whispered to himself, "I can see them."

Chapter 14

In the command tower of the slave compound on planet Crule, Devakin was tearing apart the workstations and consoles trying to get Telgrin and one of the remaining soldiers of Helion. Telgrin had crawled deep into the wall and duct work of the command tower and worked frantically to hack the system from his handheld computer.

"Get out here, you little maggots. You've lost," growled Devakin as he pulled apart the workstations.

As he did, the lone Heliender tried to lay down cover fire while Telgrin worked. He too was taking cover under the workstations. He popped up from hiding and shot a handful of rounds at Devakin, who quickly dodged all of them. The Leviathan commander ran to him and grabbed his rifle and destroyed it in his hands. He then grabbed the Heliender and threw him to the far side of the command center where he hit the wall to the right of the elevator.

Just then the elevator door opened. Devakin turned from digging for Telgrin to find Lonan standing in the elevator with his rifle aimed at him. Lonan's eyes still were ablaze with white-hot light. Devakin ran at superhuman speed around the center console. While he did he pulled his rifle and took aim at Lonan.

As Devakin rounded the corner Lonan could see him at a slower than normal speed even though he was running at a supernatural rate. Lonan took his time and fired three hounds at Devakin. The rounds flew through the air and hit the Leviathan commander in the upper right part of his chest. They punctured his armor, went through is lower shoulder, and exited through

SEBERIAN THE GREAT GATE

the back of his body armor. The impact of these rounds was tremendous and it sent Devakin flying backward and onto the floor. He lay on the command room floor writhing in pain.

"Stop the execution now!" demanded Lonan as he walked forward, his rifle still fixed on Devakin as he lay there examining the holes in his armor.

Devakin quickly pulled his hand gun and fired three rounds at Lonan.

In his mind Lonan was able to see the rounds coming in slow motion and was able to just barely jump to the side and avoid the first two. The third round grazed his shoulder, deep enough to draw blood but not enough to stop him. As he jumped to the side he rolled on the floor and came up in a kneeling position. He fired three more rounds and hit Devakin in the side.

"Stop the execution now!" shouted Lonan.

"Lonan," yelled Telgrin from deep under the control console. "I can't find a shut off in the system."

"And you never will," said Devakin as he stood up and tried to collect himself, grinning through the pain. "Just give up. Soon your planet and your people will belong to him. You've failed."

Out in the main chamber the slaves continued closer and closer toward the lava below. Many came halfway out of their slumber and cried out for help.

Devakin took a deep breath and inhaled the red mist. The red amulet in his chest plate pulsated and grew in intensity. After taking a deep breath he let out a painful cough. A little black blood came from the corner of his mouth. "Did you think that your little plan could really defeat our massive army?" sneered Devakin.

Lonan kept his rifle fixed on the enemy as he slowly walked toward him. His mind raced as he tried to think of a way to stop the execution.

Outside in the chamber the angel Balim and the demon continued in battle. They stood ten meters apart and circled each other as they tried to collect their breath. Suddenly the demon pulled a smaller blade from behind his back and threw it at Balim, who flipped backward just in time and avoided it by only centimeters. The blade continued on through the air on a direct path toward Lonan's back.

Lonan stood in the control room with his rifle still fixed on Devakin and could not see the blade flying toward him. Suddenly his eyes filled with light, and he dove to the floor. The blade flew past his head and missed him by only centimeters.

Devakin was beginning to raise his rifle when he looked up just in time to see the blade flying through the air. He had no time to react, and the blade went directly through his neck. Devakin gasped for air and fell to his knees. He looked up at Lonan as blood began to pour down the handle of the demon blade that now stuck out from his throat.

Down in the chamber Balim threw his blade after he flipped backward to avoid the demon's attack. The sword caught the demon off guard and hit him in the lower abdomen. In a flash of light Balim flew over, grabbed his blade, pulled it out, and in one lightning-fast motion spun around and cut off the demon's head. Seconds later his body and head hit the lava below and were destroyed in a dense cloud of red mist.

Lonan ran to Devakin who still knelt taking his last breaths. "I'll take that," he said as he grabbed the key from

Devakin's belt. He then quickly placed the key in the terminal and turned off the slave rack system. Immediately they stopped, but only two meters from the lava. The heat being released from the liquid was already scorching the slaves, and they continued to scream as the racks reversed and began to move upward, pulling them away from the deadly heat.

In the command center Telgrin finally hacked the system. "I'm in!" he yelled to Lonan from under the consoles.

"Close the pits," ordered Lonan, looking down at the chamber below. He saw the racks continuing upward and the large metal plates extending out from the sides of the building that locked together and created the floor that covered the lava pits.

He then turned and walked to Devakin, who still knelt on the floor gasping for air. The flame of the demon's blade slowly extinguished. Lonan crouched down beside him and looked straight into the man's eyes.

"I guess my little planet does have a chance of beating your enormous army." Lonan smiled and patted him on the shoulder. "Enjoy your time in hell." He stood up and walked toward the elevator door.

Seconds later Devakin fell face first to the floor and released his last breath.

Telgrin crawled his way out of the console and joined Lonan in the elevator. They rode down in silence as Lonan used a rag to wipe some of the blood from his eyes. He had been beaten badly and was very sore and bloody. Telgrin watched, still clean and unharmed, with his computer in his hand. "Well, that wasn't so bad."

Lonan turned to him and said nothing.

Telgrin grinned.

Lonan threw the bloody rag at him and smiled back.

Telgrin winced in disgust.

When they reached the walkway level down below, the slave racks were still moving up and coming to a stop. The captives all looked scared and confused. They had been drugged for a long time and nearly killed, so their minds needed time to get free of the effects of the drugs.

Lonan stepped out of the elevator and addressed the crowd. "Everyone relax. We're here to save you. You're free."

As he said that the racks came to a stop and the metal floors came together and closed beneath them. The haze began to lift from their eyes as the rack system released them and they stepped down onto the floor.

They began to call to each other. "Free?" "Did you hear that?" "We're free!"

Lonan looked around and could now see the red mist, which he could not see before. It was dissolving, and as it did the collection chambers in the ceiling flickered and turned off. The crowd of slaves began to celebrate. As their cheers grew louder their joy sent out shockwaves through the air. As those waves hit the collection chambers they shattered the inner parts of it.

When the waves hit the Leviathan their movements slowed dramatically and lost all their additional power. The demons, who were still locked in sword battle with the Seberians, also felt the effects and began to writhe in pain as the shockwave hit them. They squirmed and cried out as they flew out of the building to escape the onslaught of joy and hope.

Up in the ceiling a Leviathan still battled with one of the Seberians. As the fear feeding stopped, the Leviathan slowed. Then as the wave hit him he felt the evil power pour out of him. When this happened he jumped down out of the ceiling onto the suspended walkway, turned, and ran toward the outer doors of the compound.

Down below the cheers grew louder as all the remaining Leviathan and Nemaron soldiers ran out of the building. As they left the Helienders turned their attention to helping the slaves down out of the racks.

Back on planet Helion, the Leviathan still dominated the Heliender forces. Sevran lay unconscious as a Leviathan pulled him across the ground, heading for the slave transports. Just then he woke up, struggled to free himself from the grip of the powerful Leviathan. The solider laughed as Sevran squirmed within the grasp of his strong hand.

Then a shockwave entered the atmosphere and passed across the battlefield. As it reached the Leviathan they all slowed and lost their extra power. They were no longer able to dodge the Helion rounds.

The Helienders were surprised and got a renewed burst of courage as they saw that they could finally take down their attackers. Leviathan began to fall everywhere as the Helienders hit them with the electric rounds.

The Leviathan pulling Sevran suddenly had to struggle with the weight as the shockwave hit him. Sevran noticed it and looked around to see that all the Leviathan had slowed.

"He did it. He did it," yelled Sevran as he pulled his foot from the Leviathan's grip. "It's about time," he whispered as he stood up. "What happened to your powers?"

Before the Leviathan had a chance to say anything, Sevran spin kicked him in the face and knocked him out. "Not so fast now, are you?"

On the other side of the battlefield a Leviathan was still beating his way into the top of an AUV. He was punching the top and beginning to break through when the shockwave rolled across him. He threw another punch but this time without the fear feeding power. As the punch landed on the metal hull of the AUV, a tremendous crunch sound could be heard by the Helienders on the inside of the AUV as all bones in his arm and hand broke from the impact.

The Leviathan cried out in pain, and the Helienders winced from the obviously painful blow.

Inside the Helion command center everyone stood and cheered as they saw the Leviathan slowing and the Helion forces rallying. Kilgron stood and smiled as he whispered to himself, "He did it. Our home is safe."

Back on the battlefield all the Helienders who had been taking cover in the AUVs came out and attacked the confused Leviathan soldiers.

Armon and Cloin where fighting off a group of fifteen Leviathan that had completely surrounded them. They stood back to back as they collected their breath. The Leviathan began to close in as the shockwave passed over them and they returned to human speed.

Cloin and Armon could feel and see the shockwave. They gave a quick smile to one another. Then turned and took out all fifteen Leviathan in a matter of seconds. After a whirlwind of fists and blades they stood in the center of pile of fallen enemies. They panted and labored to catch their breath as they flopped down to the ground and leaned against each other back to back.

Cloin turned to her father. "Long night."

"Yeah," said Armon as he enjoyed the sight of the Helion soldiers all around him rallying and defeating the Leviathan.

On the far side to the battlefield Eliune and his group of Seberians finished taking out all of the Nemaron field artillery cannons and tanks. Finally all the cannon shots ceased.

The Helienders rallied and the battled continued, but as the Leviathan noticed that they no longer had fear-feeding power they began to give up and retreat. More soldiers of Helion poured out of the base. A group of over one hundred Leviathan gave up and ran for a nearby forest on the side of the battlefield. A unit of Helienders pursed them until they reached the forest edge.

"Wait, wait," called out one of the Helion infantry squad leaders. "I don't think we should follow them in there. Not at this time of night."

Just then they all heard a wolf howl in the not-so-far distance.

"We'll let nature take care of them." He smiled as he said, "We'll check in on them in the morning."

Those one hundred Leviathan ran into the forest and down into a deeply wooded valley. Once they reached the bottom they stopped and crowded together in a small clearing to catch their breath. Crouched over with their hands on their knees, they looked around into the forest. As their sight adjusted to the dark, they saw glowing eyes peering from the darkness.

Suddenly the wolves howled one to another, calling in the rest of the pack. The Leviathan panicked when they heard them growl and scurried around in the darkness. They pulled their rifles and started shooting wildly at anything that moved in the dark. Then in an instant all the wolves charged at once. These were a very specific breed of mountain wolf that grew to stand nearly two meters tall. The full-grown males were massive animals and extremely effective hunting and killing machines. The Leviathan armor could not help them as the animals charged in for the kill.

From outside of the forest the Helienders could hear the men shouting and firing as well as the wolves howling. They shook their heads and winced in pain, but they turned and headed back to the battlefield.

In the air above the mountain base the Nemaron pilots continued to attack the Helion fighters and soldiers on the ground. The shockwave had passed over them but did not affect them as they were not Leviathan but just regular Nemaron soldiers. They could see their comrades running from the battle and many being corralled and taken captive.

Then the Nemaron pilots noticed a group of twenty Helion fighters returning to base. These were the fighters who had escorted the slave transports on the rescue missions. They flew in from the far side of the mountain where they had just finished their escorts.

"Unit seven to base. Requesting permission to join home air defense," radioed the Helion fighter unit leader.

"Permission granted," answered Kilgron. "Welcome home."

The Helion spacecraft turned and immediately engaged the Nemaron fighters. Within moments the enemy pilots would see that their forces where losing and quickly abandon the attack. As they retreated the Helienders were able to take down several of the ships before they left the atmosphere.

Down in the hallway of the base where the Leviathan were still working to break through the doors they were using metal bars to slowly rip them open. Just then the shockwave hit them and they lost the strength to pry the door. The Leviathan looked at each other in confusion.

Then they heard a women's voice over the com: "Mission complete. The slaves have been freed."

The Leviathan heard a mottled cheer from the other side of the door as the Helienders celebrated. Suddenly the doors opened and the Helienders opened fire with their electric rounds. The Leviathan tried to dodge, but without the fear-feeding power many were quickly knocked out and found themselves on the floor. The rest turned and ran to escape only to be caught by another unit of Helienders.

At the great gate the battle continued on in deadly sword combat. Both armies had lost many soldiers, but the demons continued to push toward the gate. Suddenly a shockwave poured over them. As it did the demons slowed to a normal speed. They reeled back in pain as the loss of power physically hurt them.

Satan pulled back from his battle with Tekel and looked up into the starlit sky. "Those useless humans failed again!"

The angels continued to fight and began to push their enemy back away from the portal. The demons were noticeably disturbed as they realized that the power of the angels was more than what they could withstand without the additional power of the fear feeding.

Suddenly a second wave passed over them all. With it they could hear and feel the cheers and hope of the freed slaves. When this happened the angels' eyes blazed with a blinding-white light.

Empowered with renewed strength, the angels rallied and pushed the demons back with power and speed that they couldn't handle. Soon the enemy began to shrink back in fear. They gave up and fled the battlefield. Half of the angels pursued them while the other half stayed to secure the gate.

"No, you fools!" howled Satan. "Don't leave, we can still defeat them!"

"It's over. You've failed," said Tekel as he stepped closer to the chief demon.

Rage welled up within Satan, and he lunged at Tekel with his blade.

Tekel deflected the strike and quickly countered the attack with a swing that just barely cut Satan's throat. Not deep enough to cause damage, but enough to draw blood.

Satan reeled back in amazement that he had been hit. It had been a long time since he had been wounded in battle. He touched his neck with his hand and then looked down to find his black blood.

"Nearly a deadly blow," said Tekel as he began to circle his foe. "A little closer and it would have been the end of you."

Satan jumped high in the air and took to flight in the opposite direction. He turned in mid-air and faced Tekel. "These humans are weak and easy to manipulate. I'll collect more of the little maggots. This battle will never end."

"You know that's not true," answered Tekel, and his voice changed. It became deeper and sounded as if hundreds of angels were speaking. "Your time here is short."

Enraged, Satan shuttered and shrunk back as he released a deep, beast-like roar. He then turned and flew off into space.

In the far outer atmosphere of the planet Helion, the Nemaron fighters turned to retreat to defensive positions in order to protect their command ships. The Helion fighters continued to work to disable as many Nemaron fighters as possible.

Several Nemaron shuttles returned from the planet and docked on different command ships. The shuttle that Averine had been loaded on landed on Maginon's command ship. As it touched down in the main hangar, the hatch opened and several high ranking officers got off the ship. A Nemaron soldier pulled Averine by the arm. She had been drugged and handcuffed so she couldn't walk or see very well.

An officer from the command ship approached them. "Take her to Maginon's chamber and get her cleaned up."

"Yes, sir."

He walked her out of the main hangar and down a corridor. Moments later they entered Maginon's chamber. The soldier walked her across the room to a door on the other side. He opened the door, removed her restraints, and shoved her into the room.

"Clean her up," he commanded the girls who were already in there.

Averine stumbled through the door as the girls slowly walked to her to give her aid. They escorted her to a cot as she looked around, trying to focus her hazy eyes. They helped her lie down and began to wash the blood and dirt from her face.

One of the women brought her a clear cup full of a green liquid. She placed it in Averine's hands. "Here, drink this."

Chapter 15

B ack on the planet Helion Sevran rode his motorcycle to the spot where Averine's AUV had been destroyed. He jumped off his bike and began frantically searching through the ruble. He found an injured Heliender pinned under part of the hull of the AUV. Sevran ran to him and started lifting ruble from his body.

"Medic!" Sevran shouted to the other soldiers nearby. "You're going to be ok. Just lie still. Have you seen Averine?"

Three combat medics ran over to help the soldier. They began carefully pulling debris from his body as he labored reply. "They took her to one of their shuttles."

Sevran looked up toward the Nemaron side of the battlefield where the Helion forces where taking the remaining Nemaron soldiers captive.

"Ok, hang in there, we've got you," said Sevran. He turned and jumped on his bike and rode off toward the Nemaron shuttles.

Sevran quickly rode toward the Nemaron lines. Moments later he arrived at the Nemaron camp to find the Helion forces taking the Nemaron soldiers captive. The Leviathan had lost most of their power and speed, so the electric rounds and nets made it far easier for the Helienders to apprehend them. Once the Leviathan had lost the fight, the rest of the regular Nemaron soldiers surrendered without much resistance. Several of the Nemaron shuttles still sat on the ground with all their pilots and soldiers kneeling outside in restraints.

Sevran searched for the Helion infantry commander and found him near the center the cluster of Nemaron shuttles and cannons. "Have you seen Averine?" he asked the commander.

"No, we haven't. My men are still searching the shuttles."

Just then one of the lieutenants approached and reported in. "Sir, we've searched all enemy craft. One of our men saw Averine being taken captive, but we haven't found her."

"She must have been aboard one of the shuttles that got away," answered the commander.

"No!" grunted Sevran as he grabbed his com. "Base, come in. Averine is not here. She's been taken captive."

Back in the Helion base, Kilgron hung his head. With deep apprehension in his eyes he looked up at the main screen and watched as the computer tracked the Nemaron command ship flying away from their planet.

All of the remaining enemy ships started their pre-light-speed acceleration. Moments later they each disappeared from the Helion surveillance system's sight and exited the star system at light speed.

"The Nemaron command ship has already left our orbit. We're too far way to reach her in time." He grabbed a com device. "Lonan, come in."

Seconds later he radioed back. "Yeah, I'm here. Is everything ok? Did it work?"

"Yeah, the base is safe, but Averine is not. She was taken captive and is now aboard one of the Nemaron command ships. They've passed too far out of our range. You'll need to intercept them. You're her only hope."

Just outside the slave compound Lonan closed his eyes and bowed his head, trying to process what he had just heard. Telgrin stood nearby and listened as the Helienders loaded the slaves into the shuttle.

"I'm taking a fighter now. Send me the co-ordinates," demanded Lonan. He set down the com and ran out the shuttle door.

Telgrin followed behind. "I'm going with you."

"Fine! Let's go."

They climbed into the cockpit of the nearest Helion fighter and within moments were in the air. Once they reached the planet's outer atmosphere Lonan piloted the ship into the correct coordinates that the Helion base had sent him. Seconds later he fired the main engines, which shoved both of them back in their seats. Then the secondary engines fired and they launched into light speed and out of the star system.

In the slave girls' room beside Maginon's chambers, Averine was finally starting to feel her head clear, which also resulted in an intense headache. She sat up in her cot and held her head in her hands.

One of the other girls tried to comfort her. "Don't worry. The sickness will leave you soon."

"Were am I?" Averine asked as she rubbed her temples.

"We're in the private chambers of Maginon."

"We've got to get out of here," said Averine. She looked around to find nine other women in the room. Each of them looked healthy, but the look on their faces showed that they had lost all hope. Many had been a captive to Maginon for several months. They were all filled with a great deal of fear. If their captor grew tired of them they were taken away and never to be seen again. No one knew where they were taken, but they knew that it could not be good.

Averine's mind immediately went to work trying to figure out an escape plan.

"How? The door is locked."

"Those who resist are beaten," answered anther girl from the other side to the room.

"Or worse," said the girl nearest to her as she handed her another cup of the green liquid. "Here. This will help clear your head of the drugs."

On the other end of the ship Maginon walked down the corridor when one of his officers met him. "Your orders, sir?"

"Get us as far away from this solar system as possible. Set your course to our nearest stronghold. We'll re-group there."

"Yes, sir."

"And have some entrainment prepared for me in my chambers."

"Of course, sir."

In the girls' chambers they had all gathered around Averine and listened intently as she whispered.

"But even if we do get out of here, how will we get off this ship?"

"We can steal one of theirs and I'll fly us home," answered Averine.

"But the guards are so strong and they are everywhere. How can we get past them?" one of the girls asked.

"We have to fight! Fight for our lives. The next time they open that door we're going for it. I'll start, but you have to follow my lead. Okay?"

The rest of the girls reluctantly shook their heads in agreement.

Just then the door opened and one of the guards walked in.

"Whose turn is it tonight?" asked the guard as he grinned and looked around the room. His eyes settled on Averine. "Maginon wants someone fresh. You, come here," he said as he pointed at Averine.

"No, thanks. I would rather stay here with my new friends."

"I don't think so," said the guard. He walked toward Averine.

As she lay on the cot he reached out to grab her. Then with one swift motion she kicked him in the side of the knee. His leg crumbled as he dropped to the floor and cried out in pain. He reached for her again. She grabbed his arm, flipped him over and pinned his arm behind his back. She did this with so much force and speed that his arm snapped. He cried out again as the rest of the girls ran to help. They jumped on him and began to tie him up and gag his mouth.

"Good job. Let's get out of here," said Averine as she turned and walked through the open door.

As she did Maginon suddenly grabbed her from behind and put her in a headlock. She kicked and struggled as she gasped for air.

"Where do you think you're going?"

"Home," Averine labored to say.

Just then she flipped him over her head. He hit the floor but quickly rolled and jumped back to his feet.

"You have some energy," Maginon said with a grin. "I like that."

He lunged at her, but she quickly took him to the ground with a throw and kicked him in the head in the process.

The rest of the girls came to the open door. Maginon pulled a pistol and stumbled to his feet while holding his throbbing head. "Enough!" he yelled. "All of you back in your room. And you," he pointed the pistol at Averine, "into my chamber."

One of the girls ran toward the open door on the other side of the room. Maginon turned and fired a round. She hit the floor.

Averine took the opportunity and pulled a small knife from her boot and threw it at Maginon. The blade punctured the wrist of his hand holding the pistol.

He dropped the gun and yelled out in pain.

Averine quickly ran to him, stunned him with a kick in the face, and then hit him with a clear and hard kick to the groin that sent him to his knees. Averine gave him one more kick in the head and knocked him unconscious.

"Quick, help me tie him up and lock him in his chamber. Everyone will think he is busy with us. That should buy us some time."

The girls ran to her side and began to tie him up.

Meanwhile all the Nemaron command ships dropped out of light speed in the system where they had been hiding before the attack. They hovered in space as Maginon's command ship navigated down through the heavy meteor belt. As it neared the planet the ship moved into a large clearing that offered a great deal of natural protection from the massive meteors that orbited the planet.

The rest of the remaining carriers continued on out of the star system. They had been given orders to return to their respective bases in nearby galaxies in order to collect fresh legions of soldiers and heavy equipment.

Just then Lonan and Telgrin dropped out of light speed a great distance outside of their system. They slowly approached the planet and its ring of enormous meteors.

"We're going into stealth mode," said Lonan as he piloted.

Telgrin navigated from the co-pilot's seat. He flipped some switches and their fighter disappeared from view.

"Can you pick up her frequency yet?" asked Lonan.

"No, not yet. Wait, yes. She is definitely on the command shuttle," said Telgrin; he pointed to Maginon's space craft in the center of the meteor cluster.

"Find me an empty hangar," said Lonan as he continued toward the outer edge of the meteor belt.

"Far side, second from last one, and it's close to Averine's signal. I'm not picking up many soldiers. Looks like they are down to skeleton crew."

"He must have abandoned most of his men on Helion."

Lonan carefully piloted his ship up and under the Nemaron command shuttle and landed in the empty hangar.

"Hack their system and keep them out of this hangar," said Lonan as he brought the fighter in for a landing.

"I am already on it, boss," answered Telgrin. He worked feverishly, digging his way through the Nemaron computer system.

As he worked a probe dropped down out of the bottom side of the fighter. It landed on the floor of the hangar and began drilling its way through the metal floor. Once through the floor the probe opened to reveal small robotic arms that pushed and pulled it through the maze of wires and tubes. It searched until it found main cables to attach itself to. Now that it was connected Telgrin was able to have direct access and therefore able to hack the Nemaron system more quickly.

Lonan jumped out of the pilot's seat, gathered some weapons, and opened the main hatch of the fighter.

"I'm in," said Telgrin. "Wow, that was fast."

Just as Lonan prepared to step off the ship and into the hangar the Nemaron alarm system sounded.

"Great!" Lonan yelled over the alarm. "That'll make this easier."

"Sorry."

"Just man the guns and do whatever you need to do to keep them off me."

"You got it."

Lonan turned and ran off the fighter, through the hangar, and down the hallway. He looked down at his tracking device, which displayed the ship's layout. On it he could also see a blinking green dot indicating his wife's location.

"Great, she is on the move," said Lonan. He picked up the pace and ran down the hall.

Elsewhere on the ship Averine and the other girls quietly peeked through the door of Maginon's chamber and into the hallway. Averine motioned for the rest to follow as she turned to her left.

Running down the hall with his eyes scanning in all directions for Nemaron soldiers, Lonan glanced down at his tracking device to see that Averine had turned in the opposite direction and was now moving away from him.

"No, wrong way. Come back this way," Lonan whispered to himself as he changed to an all-out sprint. In moments he ran past the main door to Maginon's chamber where Averine and the girls had been seconds before. Lonan reached the end of the hall and turned left to follow Averine's signal.

Only seconds after Lonan turned the corner and continued running down the hall, Satan flew through the hull of the ship and into the hallway directly in front of the door to Maginon's chamber. Satan walked through the door and into the main room. He looked around and found no one and turned to enter the bed chamber. There he found Maginon laying on the floor tied and gagged and just coming to.

"What a surprise, you pitiful little fool," grumbled Satan. He pulled a blade and cut the restraints from Maginon's hands and feet.

Maginon jumped up and pulled the gag from his mouth. "I'm glad you are —"

Before he could finish Satan picked him up by his throat and threw him into the other room and against the wall. Satan slowly walked into the main chamber.

"How did you fail me with all of the men, resources, and power that I gave you?"

Maginon tried to collect himself as he stumbled to his feet. "I did exactly what you told me to do."

"Don't try to blame me for your stupidity," Satan yelled as he picked him up and threw him across the room again.

Maginon's body bounced off the wall and hit the floor. He spit blood from his mouth as he picked himself up again. Once to his feet he pleaded. "My lord, it's not all lost. We can gather more men and slaves."

Meanwhile, not far from Maginon's chamber, Averine and the girls continued to sneak down the hallway until five Nemaron soldiers appeared from around a corner.

"Hey, you there. Stop!" the soldiers yelled as they ran toward the girls with their rifles lifted and ready to shoot.

The girls turned to run the other way when suddenly a burst of rounds flew over their heads and hit the Nemaron soldiers. They all dropped to the floor, convulsing from the electrical shock.

The girls looked up to see Lonan standing above them with is rifle aimed at the enemy soldiers. He turned to Averine and hugged and kissed her.

"Come on, follow me. You're going the wrong way," said Lonan as he took Averine's hand and raced down the hallway. "As usual," he whispered under his breath.

"What?" asked Averine.

"Nothing. Let's go," answered Lonan as he led the girls back to the hangar and their waiting ship.

Moments later they ran past Maginon's chamber. As they did Lonan could sense a great deal of evil. The door was still open, and as Lonan ran past he caught a glimpse of Satan holding Maginon in the air by his throat. Lonan stopped immediately and peered into the room. He was amazed at what he could see.

Averine noticed that he had stopped. She turned back and whispered, "Lonan! What are you doing?"

He stepped toward her, handing her the tracking device and pistol.

"Here, take this. The hangar is just down that hall. Telgrin is waiting. Get everyone loaded; I'm right behind you."

"What? Why? Where are you going?" asked Averine. She looked in the chamber and saw nothing. Her eyes were not capable of seeing Satan, so she had no idea what Lonan was doing.

"Just go. I'll meet you there," whispered Lonan as he pointed her down the hall.

Averine turned and ran in the direction of the hangar as the girls followed.

Lonan pulled his rifle from his back, turned and entered through the door, his eyes blazing white.

Inside the room Satan held Maginon off the floor by the throat while he kicked and gasped for air.

"Worthless human. You've outlived your usefulness to me." Satan's eyes burned with a red haze. His mind was filled with so much rage that he gripped Maginon with this powerful hands and tore the man's body in half. He then threw his torso against one wall and his legs against the opposite. Maginon's eyes rolled back in his head as he exhaled his last breath, lying on the floor bleeding to death.

Lonan walked into the room with his rifle fixed on Satan. "Hey! I want to talk to you!"

Satan slowly turned as Lonan took short, careful steps in his direction.

"I'm here to warn you. Stay away from my family and my people."

Satan slowly drew his flaming sword. "How dare you threaten me, maggot." He stepped toward Lonan as he slowly became invisible.

Lonan followed him with his rifle. "I can still see you," said Lonan as his eyes blazed white.

Satan lunged in attack. In Lonan's mind everything went into slow motion — he could see Satan flying through the air with blade lifted high. Lonan squeezed the trigger and sent three rounds toward the demon. Each of them passed through Satan's armor and entered his chest. The heavenly rounds sent his body flying backward and writhing in pain.

"How did you do that?" grunted Satan after his body hit the back wall of Maginon's chambers.

"Like I said. I can see you now. I'm warning you, stay away from my family," threatened Lonan. He stepped forward with his rifle and white eyes still fixed on the demon.

Satan looked down to see black blood pouring from the holes in his chest plate. His eyes blazed with red fury as he jumped into the air, let out a horrific roar, and charged at Lonan.

Lonan fired three more rounds. They hit the demon in the chest and stopped him for a moment.

Satan raised his sword and charged again when suddenly an arrow pierced his hand, which caused him to drop his sword. The arrow was attached to a rope that was suddenly pulled backward, which sent Satan to the floor with a violent jerk. He cried out in pain as he turned to see the angel Balim standing behind him.

Balim stood holding his bow and the other end of the rope. "Get your people home safely," said Balim as he dropped the rope and drew his sword.

Lonan nodded to the angel, turned, and ran out the door and down the hall toward the hangar.

Satan slowly stood. He broke the arrow and pulled it from his hand. "Don't you get tired of protecting these little fools?"

"If you would leave them alone I wouldn't have to."

"Oh, but their fear, their bitterness, and their hatred tastes so good."

"Go back to your hole in the ground before I bring other warriors to escort you there."

"Enjoy your small victory... servant. I'm weak now, but I'll regain my strength and then you and the rest of the wretched faithful will die!"

Balim lost his patience. He took a step forward. With eyes blazing white he lifted his head and spoke out loudly in an angel tongue.

Satan winced in pain at the sound and pulled back three steps. Then he leapt into the air and took to flight. "Enough! I leave you. But remember that my forces are everywhere, and we will rise again." He then turned and flew through the hull of the ship and out into the pitch black of space.

Back in the hangar Telgrin sat at the co-pilot station working at a computer terminal. "Yes! Compulsion system. Let's see what damage we can cause."

Just then his computer showed ten Nemaron soldiers running down the hall about to enter the hangar. As they entered an automated gun dropped down from the bottom side of the fighter. It turned, fired electric rounds, and took out all of the soldiers as they entered.

The action startled Telgrin; he looked up from his hacking work to see the ten soldiers convulsing on the floor. "Nice work, computer. It's a good thing one of us is paying attention."

Then the computer showed Averine's I.D. signature running down the hallway with the rest of the girls behind her. Seconds later they ran into the hangar. Slowing down only to step over the pile of Nemaron soldiers, they ran to the ship to find Telgrin at the bottom of the ramp waiting for them.

"Good to see you alive. Where's Lonan?"

"He stopped for some reason."

Lonan ran into the hangar and jumped over the soldiers as he yelled, "Load up! Let's get out of here."

The girls shuffled into the small storage compartment in the back of the fighter. Lonan jumped into the pilot's seat as ten more Nemaron soldiers entered the hangar. They immediately opened fire and hit the hull of the ship only to quickly be gunned down by the automated weapon on the bottom of the Helion fighter.

"I have our exit strategy figured out," said Telgrin as Lonan lifted the fighter off the landing platform.

"Mind telling me about it?"

"Get us out of here and I'll show you," said Telgrin.

The ship turned and blasted out of the hangar.

Chapter 16

Lonan piloted the fighter away from the command ship. As he did more Nemaron soldiers entered the hangar and fired hundreds of rounds at the escaping Helienders. Within seconds the command ship's cannons turned and took aim.

Averine turned on the targeting system and fired a group of rounds at the canons. She quickly took out one, but the other fired multiple shoots at the fighter as it gained speed and pulled away from the enemy ship.

Telgrin continued to work at his computer station as Lonan piloted the spacecraft.

"Get ready for a show!" grinned Telgrin as he finished punching some keys.

Deep inside the Nemaron command ship, the main engines began to overheat. Soldiers scurried as the nearby computer monitors signaled a warning of the temperature levels.

On the command deck the pilots also saw the engine warnings. "Sir, we have a problem," reported one of the soldiers.

The captain turned. "What's going on? Stabilized those engines."

"I can't sir! There not responding! I'm locked out of the system!"

In the Helion fighter Telgrin watched the engines with a wide grin on his face as they flew away from the command ship.

The engines of the Nemaron ship exploded in four enormous balls of fire. This caused them to lose all power inside the command ship. All the lights went out and low lever emergency lighting came on. The main body of the ship was still intact, but all propulsion had ceased and the ship floated helplessly through space.

Telgrin jumped and cheered. "Yes! They won't be getting away."

"Nice work," said Lonan. "I knew there was a reason I brought you."

Back at planet Helion the shuttles had returned from the rescue missions. They had landed outside of the base and hundreds of freed slaves were helped off the shuttles by Helion soldiers and medics. Some had to be carried off in stretchers. They were all very weak and malnourished, but they all were very relieved to have been freed.

Off in the distance the Helienders continued to collect and restrain the enemy soldiers. They loaded the weakened Leviathan into prison transports and hauled them away to shuttles that were waiting on the far side of the battlefield. They would be taken to a nearby planet where they would be housed in a Helion restoration facility. There they would be helped with their physical and psychological problems as the evil Leviathan poisons were cleansed from their bodies.

Sevran, Armon, Cloin, and Eluine stood outside the base watching as an attractive young woman medic tended to Sevran's wounded arm.

Kilgron walked out of the main hangar and joined the group.

"We just received word from your brother. They are all safe and will be arriving soon," reported Kilgron.

"I knew he'd pull it off."

"I trust you'll survive your wounds," said Kilgron as he examined Sevran's arm.

"Yes, sir. I'm getting great medical attention here," said Sevran as he winked at the young medic.

She looked up at him and smiled.

Cloin rolled her eyes.

"Don't milk it. We have work to do. Many repairs to be made to the base," said Kilgron. He looked down over the battlefield that was filled with destroyed AUVs, Stingers, and Nemaron tanks. He could also see the enormous smoking hole that had been blown in the side of the base.

"Yes, sir."

One of the freed slaves walked over to Sevran. She was a frail older woman who could barely walk. She reached out and hugged him around his waist. "Thank you so much for saving us," she said with a tear in her eye.

"We're glad to help," said Sevran. He smiled and kissed her on the top of her white head.

Cloin tried to hide a smile as a medic came and escorted the woman into the base.

"This way, ma'am. You need to be seen by one of our doctors."

Just then Lonan's fighter came into view and landed on the outer edge of the landing pad. As the ramp of the fighter opened, Averine and Telgrin led the girls out.

Averine turned to Telgrin. "Can you show them to the medical bay?"

"Sure. This way ladies," answered Telgrin.

Averine turned and walked to her father and the others.

"I'm so glad you're safe," said Kilgron as he hugged his daughter. He felt the deepest sense of relief as he held her.

Averine turned to Sevran and patted him directly on the bandage of his arm. He winced in pain. "Ouch! Bandage."

"Oh, you're fine," said Averine as she watched Lonan walk toward the group. "I'm going to help in the medical unit."

As he approached the group Averine reached out and hugged her husband. "I'll see you inside later. I'm going to help with the wounded."

"Okay," answered Lonan before he turned to Sevran and lightly hit his brother's bandaged arm.

"Good to see you in one piece."

Sevran winced again in pain and said, "Same to you," as he punched Lonan in the shoulder. "I'm going inside to find people with a little more compassion."

"Good luck," answered Lonan with a grin.

Sevran stood and began to walk toward the hangar door. As he did four young women came out to greet him. As soon as he saw them he began to fake a slight limp. The girls gathered around him and helped him into the base.

"Are you ok?" one of them asked.

"Yeah, sure. I'll be fine."

"Let us help you," another said.

The four girls came along beside him and helped him limp into the base.

Lonan shook his head in disgust. "Faker."

Telgrin guided the girls who had been held captive by Maginon through the main hangar.

"This way, ladies," he said as he looked up just in time to see that they were walking past Sarah, who was attending to a wounded soldier. She was the young medic that Telgrin secretly loved but could never seemed to muster the strength to talk to for more than five seconds.

Sarah turned just as she was finishing with the soldier and saw Telgrin walking in with the group of women.

"Did you rescue these people?" Sarah asked with a brilliant smile.

"Sort of...I mean... yes," stumbled Telgrin. "We rescued them from Maginon himself. Well, I didn't. I was just a part of the mission." Telgrin fumbled around as he tried not to make too much eye contact.

"You were on their main command ship?"

"Yes, I was," answered Telgrin with some renewed boldness as he saw that she seemed to be impressed. "In fact, I hacked their system and destroyed their engines. They're just floundering up there in space waiting for us to go haul them to the dungeons."

"Wow. I'm impressed," Sarah answered with a shy glint in her eye.

A group of rescued slaves from the planet Crule compound shuffled by on their way to the medial bay. One of them was a man who had been separated from his wife on the planet Tarnus. She was a beautiful young woman and had been taken to Maginon's chambers. She was now walking in the same hangar with the group of women and Telgrin. The man was shuffling along still trying to recover from the drugs of the slave compound. He looked up for a second and happened to see his wife in the other group.

"Clarine!" he yelled as he shoved his way through the crowd. "Clarine!"

She looked up immediately as she recognized his voice. They ran to one another and meet in the middle of the hangar. Tears began to flow down their faces as they shared a much-needed embraced.

"Are you ok?" asked the man as he looked her over.

"Yes, yes," she answered through tears. "But I never thought I would see you again."

Sarah turned to Telgrin and whispered, "Nice work."

"Yeah. I guess so," answered Telgrin as he turned away a little in a futile attempt to hide the fact that his eyes were tearing up.

Meanwhile, just outside the main hangar, Kilgron placed his hand on Lonan's shoulder. "You and your teams did a great job. You've saved our people and helped to put an end to a terrible reign of evil men."

As he spoke a little girl from the slave camp was walking off the transport. She smiled at Lonan and waved. He smiled and waved back.

Tekel, Balim and Genon flew down and landed beside Lonan and the others. Balim nodded in Lonan's direction. Armon turned to the angels and said, "Thank you for your help."

"This is only a temporary victory," answered Tekel. "Satan will be back. He will cower in this cave as he heals. He has other armies of men in other galaxies, and he will gather his demons to him once again."

"But Maginon is dead. I saw Satan kill him."

"It doesn't matter," added Balim. "He'll enslave another pawn to do his will."

"We need to go and warn other solar systems," said Lonan.

"You're right," responded Armon. "If they are prepared, there'll be less destruction."

Cloin added, "We need to train more Seberians. God has told me that the time has come."

"Yes," answered Tekel as he and other angels nodded in agreement.

"This war was been going on for millennia," added Balim. "But it will end one day."

As he spoke things began to stir in heaven. He and the other angels could see the heavenly activity in their minds eye. They could see, one by one, their angel brothers who had been killed in these recent wars appearing alive in heaven.

Meanwhile back at the great gate, the doors suddenly opened a small amount and an immense heavenly white light poured into creation.

In a brilliantly lit chamber in the heart of heaven a man knelt on the floor covered in a simple, brown hooded cape. He knelt motionless with his head hung low and two blades sheathed on his back. Suddenly his head lifted, his eyes opened, and a blinding-white light radiated from under the hood of his cape.

Tekel and the other angels smiled as they saw this man in preparation.

"God is preparing his ultimate warrior," said Tekel. "He is the original soldier of hope, the original Seberian. He is far more powerful than any us, and He will end this war for all time."

Here ends the second part of Seberian Series and the history of the battle at the Great Gate and the defense of the planet Helion. The third part chronicles the coming of the greatest of the Soldiers of Hope in Seberian, Declaration of War.

NOTE FROM THE AUTHOR,

I really hope that you're enjoying the Seberian Series. This story is pre-Messiah, but he is coming. My hope in writing this story was to go back to beginning and re-tell the fall of creation from a fresh science fiction perspective. It seems sometimes that telling a story from a parallel perspective can make it more understandable or fresh.

The goal that I feel that God has given me in this is to show that there is a spiritual battle going on and that He is still on our side. And most importantly that He sent Jesus to "destroy the devil's work," (I John 3:8) and that we have victory over the enemy through Jesus. That is where this story is going.

As I mentioned before this project started as a movie script and it's our goal to produce it as a live-action feature length film. The angel character Tekel that you see on the cover is one of the props that we built.

To find out more about the project please join the Seberian Nation (e-mail newsletter) and check out the website.

SEBERIAN.COM

You can also go back to the beginning of the book and check out the "Word from the author" *section.*

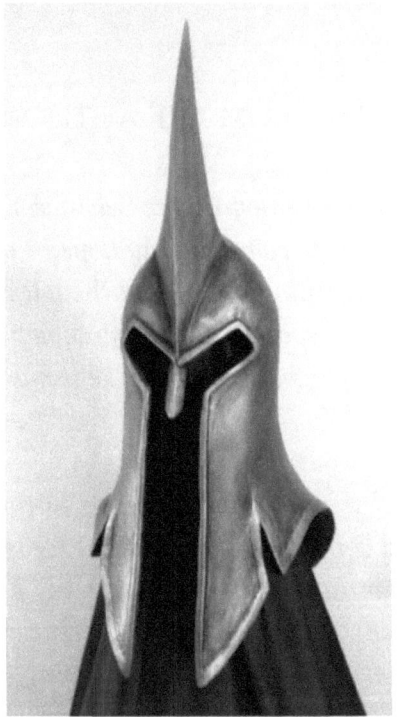

Tekel's Helmet
Designed & built by Jason Dahl
Step 1 = sculpted in clay
Step 2 = rotaional casing in plastic

Conceptual art for armor by
Rob Richardson

Armor built by Jason Dahl
Based on Rob's conceptual drawings.
(Make shift photoshoot in Jason's dining room.

Yes, his wife loved that.)

Find out the backstory of the Helion people when you download the prequel for free!
Seberian, The Beginning.

Check out our website **SEBERIAN.COM** and…

- **Download a FREE COPY of the prequel,**
- Learn more about the book & movie project,

Also, if you could do a review on Amazon, I would really appreciate it. They help A LOT.

Thanks,
Jason Dahl.

SPECIAL THANKS

I want to give a HUGE special thanks to some very cool people who helped to get this book out.

Bonneta & Charles
Mindy & Phil
Marilyn & Doug
Sandy
Jordan
Sarah

Thank you so much for your support. You guys rock!
Jason.

www.ingramcontent.com/pod-product-compliance
Lightning Source LLC
Chambersburg PA
CBHW032145170626
46808CB00006B/2379